SOLD TO
THE SHEIKH

BY
MIRANDA LEE

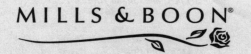

MILLS & BOON®

First published in Great Britain 2003
Harlequin Mills & Boon Limited,
Eton House, 18-24 Paradise Road, Richmond, Surrey TW9 1SR

© Miranda Lee 2003

ISBN 0 263 83711 4

Set in Times Roman 10½ on 12 pt.
01-0204-46339

Printed and bound in Spain
by Litografía Rosés, S.A., Barcelona

'You think I just *desire* you?'

She bristled at his attempt to deny that his interest in her was strictly sexual. 'I *know* you just desire me, your highness. You made me brutally aware of your lust from the first moment we met. It knocked you for six when I turned your dinner invitation down, so much so that when you got the chance you paid five million dollars to force me to do what I told you I would never do willingly. But there is nothing you can say or do to make me change my mind about what kind of man you are. I already know what kind you are. I've met your kind before.'

'Oh, I doubt that, dear lady,' he said in a tone that sent shivers running up and down her spine. 'In that case,' he ground out, 'you leave me no alternative.'

Charmaine swallowed. 'What do you mean? No alternative…?'

A prickling sensation ran over her skin. Whatever he was about to say, Charmaine knew she wasn't going to like it.

'I paid five million dollars for a few short hours of your company tonight. I will donate five *hundred* million dollars to your precious charity foundation…if you spend a week with me.'

Three Rich Men…

*Three Australian billionaires: they can have anything,
anyone…except three beautiful women…*

Meet Charles, Rico and Ali, three incredibly wealthy
friends all living in Sydney. They meet every Friday
night to play poker and exchange news, about business
and their pleasures—which include the pursuit of
Sydney's most beautiful women.

Up until now, no single woman has ever managed to
pin down the elusive, exclusive and eminently eligible
bachelors. But that's about to change. First Charles,
then Rico and finally Ali fall for three gorgeous girls…

But will these three rich men marry for love—
or are they desired for their money…?

Recent titles by the same author:

AT HER BOSS'S BIDDING

Three Rich Men

A RICH MAN'S REVENGE
MISTRESS FOR A MONTH
SOLD TO THE SHEIKH

PROLOGUE

HIS eyes had been on her all afternoon. Dark, beautiful eyes. Arrogant eyes. Presumptuous eyes.

Charmaine knew, soon after their introduction, that His Royal Highness, Prince Ali of Dubar, was going to make some kind of pass before the day's races were over.

From the moment she became aware of the sheikh's interest in her, Charmaine regretted accepting this particular job. The pleasure of being one of the judges for the 'Fashion-in-the-Field' competition during Flemington's spring racing carnival did not override the displeasure of being pursued by yet another international playboy.

But by the time she'd completed the job she'd been hired for—the final judging on Ladies' Day had been over by four—Charmaine had a firm handle on her irritation and began looking forward to that moment when her admirer put his mouth where his eyes had been, so to speak. Not literally, of course. The thought of such a man actually kissing her made her shudder. Nothing repelled Charmaine more than overly good-looking, overly wealthy men who thought any female they fancied could be had for the price of a dinner. Or even less.

And this one was more than overly good-looking and overly wealthy. The Arab prince and horse breeder was one of the most handsome men—and undoubtedly one of the richest—Charmaine had ever

met. Taller and leaner in her opinion than most Arab princes, he was also clean-shaven and dressed that day not in traditional Arab dress, but a pale grey suit and brilliant white shirt which highlighted his richly olive skin and thick, jet-black hair. His face was as hard and lean as his body, his dark, deeply set eyes bisected by a strong nose that was underlined by a cruelly carved but not unattractive mouth.

He looked unlike any sheikh Charmaine had ever met. And she'd met a few. Supermodels met many of the world's wealthiest men, both in the course of their careers and their social lives. The rich and famous liked having the bold and the beautiful at their dos.

Being invited to be a special guest of Prince Ali in his private box at the races had not surprised Charmaine. Having the sheikh think what he had obviously been thinking about her all afternoon didn't surprise her, either. In her experience, billionaire Arab playboys had a tendency to overestimate their own irresistibility, as well as underestimate the morals of some western women. No doubt, in this sheikh's mind, supermodel equated with superslut.

Charmaine would take great delight in cutting Prince Ali down to size a little. His inflated male ego, she decided as she sensed him watching her again, needed pruning.

She was right. He *was* watching her, his eyes never leaving her as she made her way back up into the stand, burning their way through her figure-hugging silk dress, stripping her of every stitch and leaving her feeling stark naked and almost bitter over her undeniable physical assets. Not for the first time, Charmaine had a moment of burning resentment over the genes which had combined her father's height and

Nordic fairness with her mother's large blue eyes and womanly curves to produce a tall, head-turning blonde who'd first rocketed to modelling fame at the tender age of sixteen.

Nine years later, Charmaine's precocious beauty had blossomed into a more mature but still widely recognisable look with her striking figure and extra-long but perfectly straight fair hair. Hourglass shapes were supposedly out of fashion, but Charmaine's elegantly elongated version was eagerly sought after by designers, primarily because she could showcase their wares more effectively than her thinner colleagues. She was especially popular with swimwear and lingerie fashion houses and had made a small fortune being photographed in a state of dishabille.

Unfortunately, a side-effect of being seen on billboards and magazine covers in skimpy underwear and hardly there bikinis was that some men presumed her whole body was for sale, not just the image she projected. It was amazing how many wealthy men had thought they could buy her as their trophy girlfriend, or mistress, or even wife. Charmaine found this perversely amusing. Little did they know but she was the last woman on earth they would want in their beds.

The man staring at her at this moment would be severely disappointed if she agreed to whatever of those three intimate alternatives he had in mind. She was actually doing him a favour in rejecting his overtures.

With a small smile hovering on her lips, she lowered herself with an almost perverse pleasure into the seat he'd obviously kept clear for her, right next to his own and close enough for her to smell his expen-

sive cologne and see that his black eyes were framed with the longest lashes she had ever seen on a man.

The rest of the box was empty, not even graced by the granite-faced bodyguard who'd either stood at the back or shadowed the prince everywhere he'd gone so far that afternoon. Clearly the bodyguard had encountered this particular scenario before, and knew to make himself scarce whilst his boss chatted up whatever lady his royal eye had fallen upon.

'I have been eagerly awaiting your return,' the prince said in that overly formal manner which only a British private-school education could have instilled in him. 'You have finished your judging for today?'

'Yes, thank goodness. I didn't realise how difficult a task it would be, picking the winner from so many beautifully dressed ladies.'

'If I had been the judge, there would have been only the one winner. And that is your lovely self.'

Oh, *please*, she thought wearily. Save it for a more impressed model.

Charmaine didn't give voice to her irritation. Not yet. Instead, she waited patiently for him to put his foot further into his mouth.

'I was wondering if you might be free this evening,' he went on predictably. 'I would very much like to have your company at dinner.'

What you'd like, my pompous prince, is to have *me* for dinner. Or afters.

Her eyes turned cold as his continued to smoulder.

'I'm sorry,' she returned with an upward tilt of her chin that lifted the brim of her picture hat and gave him a clearer view of her icy blue eyes, 'but I'm not free tonight.'

Her first refusal did not deter him, as she knew it wouldn't.

'Perhaps another night, then. I hear you live in Sydney. You may not be aware of the fact, but I am in Sydney every weekend.'

Actually, she hadn't been aware of much about the prince at all till today. Like a lot of sheikhs, he did not seek publicity. But a Melbourne racehorse-owning couple who were also guests of the prince today had been more than happy to fill her in when he was off presenting a trophy for one of the early races which his family had sponsored. Charmaine now knew he was in his mid-thirties and managed a huge thoroughbred stud in the upper Hunter Valley north-west of Sydney, a job he'd been doing very successfully for the last decade. Apparently, his royal family's interests in horse-racing spread far and wide and they had similar breeding establishments in Britain and America. Prince Ali, however, was solely in charge of the Australian branch.

She'd also been discreetly informed of his reputation as a ladies' man and a lover, although she wasn't sure if that had been a warning or an advertisement for her host's boudoir skills, a teaser meant to whet her appetite to experience the reality rather than the rumour. If so, his minions had been wasting their time. They'd definitely picked the wrong target today. And so had he.

She couldn't wait to enlighten him of his mistake.

'I will be back in Sydney by tomorrow afternoon,' he went on suavely, his eyes never leaving hers. 'I play cards with friends in my hotel suite every Friday night and attend the Sydney races every Saturday. To be truthful I rarely travel interstate. I only came to

Melbourne this week because I had a horse running in the Cup last Tuesday and another in the Oaks today. Unfortunately, neither of them won.'

'How sad for you,' she said without a trace of true sympathy in her voice.

He didn't seem to notice, however. Perhaps he could not conceive of the possibility that a woman would not hang on his every word, or feel anything but flattery over his obvious interest.

Charmaine almost smiled over the thought that Prince Ali of Dubar was about to have a new experience with the opposite sex. It was called…rejection.

'Would you be free to go to dinner with me this Saturday night?' he persisted, as she had known he would. 'Or do you have further commitments which will keep you down here in Melbourne?'

'No. I fly back to Sydney tomorrow morning. But I won't be free to have dinner with you that night, either. Sorry,' she added blithely.

His frown carried some confusion. 'You have another engagement?'

'No,' came her succinct reply.

His frown deepened. 'There is a lover who would object to your going out to dinner with me?' he ventured in his bewilderment. 'Or a secret patron perhaps?'

Charmaine's irritation reached new heights, prompted by both his stuffy manner of speech and his presumption that there had to be some man stopping her from going out with him. It could not possibly be that she *didn't* find him irresistible and didn't *want* to go out with him. What annoyed her most, however, was his last inference that she might already be some wealthy man's secret mistress.

'I have no lover, or *patron*, as you put it,' she replied curtly. 'The fact is, your royal highness, I will *never* be free to go out with a man like you, so please save yourself the trouble and don't ask again.'

His eyes flared momentarily with shock before going as hard as ebony, his dark brows gathering like clouds before the storm.

'A man like me,' he reiterated in clipped tones. 'Might I ask exactly what you mean by that?'

'You may ask,' she answered coolly, 'but you will not get an answer.'

'Surely I have a right to know why you have turned me down so rudely.'

Some of the fury that Charmaine had kept bottled up for years bubbled up in her throat and found voice.

'*Right?*' she snapped, and was on her feet in a flash. 'You have no *rights* where I am concerned. You asked me out. I declined. You asked me again, so I made it quite clear that any further attentions of yours are unwanted. I don't think that is rude. That is *my* right, to not be pestered by spoiled and arrogant men who have not had no said to them nearly often enough. My answer is and always will be no, Prince Ali. Hear it and take heed of it, because if you ever make contact with me again, I will have you arrested for stalking!'

She whirled and swept out of the box, swishing her way down the steps and out of the stand. She half expected him to charge after her but he didn't, for which she was grateful, because she knew if he dared lay a hand on her, she would strike him across his arrogant face. Her hands were gripping her handbag with white-knuckled intensity, but they would have loved any excuse to lash out physically at him. A

verbal assault was not nearly enough to soothe her temper.

Charmaine didn't stop her angry retreat till she had reached the car park, and her car. But even as she climbed in behind the wheel of her rented blue car and started up the engine, she was still shaking inside.

The sight of the sheikh's stunned face suddenly filled her mind and she groaned. She had gone too far this time. Way too far.

Normally, she said her nos to such men much more politely and tactfully. Something about Prince Ali, however, had brought out the worst in her. She wasn't sure what. Possibly because he was armed with far too many attractions for most females to resist. Goodness, those *eyes*!

Charmaine imagined he'd been very successful in seducing then carelessly discarding many silly Australian girls in the past. Such thoughts had her blood heating in her veins again. When she went to reverse out of her spot, she did so recklessly and almost backed into another car. She must have missed it by an inch.

Giving herself a rigorous mental shake, Charmaine forcibly calmed herself before resuming her exit from the car park. The last thing she wanted was to have an accident. She had to be in Fiji on Monday, on a photo shoot for the cover of a sporting magazine.

Stop thinking about the man, she lectured herself as she drove off at a relatively sedate speed. And stop feeling guilty. Men like him don't have feelings like ordinary people. They have egos, and desires, both of which are well catered for. So he wanted you for a moment today. And he didn't get what he wanted for once. Big deal! He won't go to dinner—or to bed—

alone tonight. There will be some other foolish female to soothe his ego and satisfy his desires. You don't have to worry about him. Or even *think* about him.

But she *did* think about him, on and off for the next week. Guilt, she supposed. Being so openly rude was not part of her usual public persona. When out and about, she kept her feelings well hidden, covering the darkness within under a cloak of sweetness and light. The way she'd treated the sheikh had been quite uncharacteristic and strangely troubling.

Finally, however, all thought of him was gone, banished from her mind as she got on with her life and her life's work. Charmaine was on a mission these days, and that mission had no time for men. Certainly not men like Prince Ali of Dubar. She'd finished with that type many years before. More recently, she'd finished with the nicer types as well.

The media would be surprised to know that Charmaine, the Aussie model who'd been voted by more than one glossy rag as one of the sexiest women in the world, now lived a celibate lifestyle. There were no boyfriends or lovers any more. And definitely no secret *patrons*, she thought sneeringly. The very idea!

Of course, Charmaine had enough business nous to realise that news of her nun-like life would not do her career any good. Being seen as sexy and sexually active was part of her image. So she continued to be snapped by the media at premières and parties on the arms of handsome young men, usually hunky male models who had a sexual secret of their own, namely that they were gay. And she continued to model the most daring of clothes, often without any visible underwear.

Charmaine kept her public profile high, and her image extremely sexy. She earned more money that way. And money was the name of the game these days. It took millions, she'd found out since she started up the Friends of Kids with Cancer foundation, to fund cancer research, as well as make the lives of children already suffering from cancer more bearable, not to mention their poor families' lives. Millions and millions!

Sometimes, Charmaine surrendered to depression over the enormity of the mission she'd set herself. Could she really make a difference? But most of the time she was filled with the most dogged determination. She would do anything she could to raise money for her own very personal cause and crusade.

Anything at all!

CHAPTER ONE

OCTOBER, the second month of spring in Sydney, eleven months later...

'I have to admire your courage, Charmaine,' Renée said as she glanced up from where she'd been studying the lunch menu. 'Have you thought about what kind of man the highest bidder for your dinner-date-with-Charmaine prize next Saturday night could be?'

'A very rich man, hopefully,' Charmaine replied with a flash of pearly white teeth. 'My total target for the banquet and auction is ten million dollars.'

'He could be a right sleazebag, you know,' Renée warned. 'Or an obsessed fan.'

Charmaine smiled again over at Renée, who was not only the owner of the modelling agency she was currently contracted to, but a nice person, too. Even nicer now that she was happily married and expecting.

As much as Charmaine was cynical when it came to rich and handsome men, she had to concede that it looked as if Renée had found a one-off in Rico Mandretti. Who would have thought that the playboy king of cable-TV cooking shows would turn out to be good husband and father material?

But he had. When Charmaine met the *A Passion for Pasta* star in person for the first time the other night, he hadn't flirted with her one bit. A good sign. Not that she could be absolutely sure of Mr

Mandretti's loyalty and sincerity, she supposed. She and Renée did not mix socially so she didn't know Renée and Rico as a couple at all. Her own relationship with Renée, though friendly, was strictly business. Charmaine never confided her personal secrets or innermost feelings to the woman.

'I don't care what kind of man he is,' Charmaine said truthfully, 'as long as he pays a good price for the privilege. You don't have to worry about my safety, Renée, though it's sweet of you to care. It is clearly stipulated on the auction programme that the dinner date is to be held the following Saturday night in the By Candlelight restaurant in the Regency Hotel, which is a public place. If there's even a hint of trouble, I'll be out of there like a shot.'

Renée had no doubt she would be, too. Charmaine was one tough cookie. Much tougher than the image she projected on the catwalk and in photographs. There, she was all soft sex kitten, her looks and manner creating an unusual combination of sensuality and innocence which always fascinated men and rarely alienated women.

Renée had often tried to analyse what exactly it was about Charmaine's looks which managed this miracle. Where *did* that air of innocence come from? Perhaps from her fresh, flawless complexion or maybe her long, straight fair hair which fell in a simple curtain to her waist. Certainly not from her full, pouty mouth, almost *too* voluptuous figure or her come-to-bed blue eyes.

The contradictory nature of Charmaine's beauty was as elusive as her inner self.

Renée suspected that no one in the modelling industry knew the real Charmaine, certainly not the

male models she occasionally dated. Renée knew for a fact that those particular pretty boys were just handbags to Charmaine, sexy accessories for public consumption. Real boyfriends they definitely were not.

Actually, in the time she'd known Charmaine, she'd never known her to have a real boyfriend. More than likely, the girl didn't have time for personal relationships these days, what with her career and her charity work. But Rico—typical testosterone-based man that he was—did not agree. He believed she'd more likely been burned by some man in the past and was going through a cynical phase. Rico had difficulty with the idea of any woman not really wanting a man in her life.

Maybe he was right. And maybe not. Renée was not about to risk her professional relationship with Charmaine by asking her questions about her sex life. She'd been over the moon when Australia's most successful model signed up with her agency eighteen months back.

Previously, Charmaine had employed a personal agent-manager, but he'd been fired after fiddling his expenses. If there was one thing that girl was ruthless about, it was her money. She demanded to be well paid and she didn't give an unnecessary cent away.

A good percentage of the money she earned, Renée suspected, went to Charmaine's beloved Friends of Kids with Cancer foundation, which she'd personally started up not long before she'd joined Renée's modelling agency. Charmaine's little sister had died of leukaemia the year before, and the tragedy had affected the girl greatly. After a couple of months' sabbatical from modelling to grieve the loss, she'd come

out fighting to do something to help other such kids. Hence, the foundation.

When Charmaine was on the fund-raising war-path, no one was safe. She harassed everyone she met for monetary donations or their time. She'd even coerced Renée into talking Rico into being the compère at the auction on Saturday night. Renée was thankfully absolved from taking part herself because she was seven months pregnant. With twins! But she would be attending, of course.

Actually, Renée was looking forward to that evening. Charles and Dominique would be there, which meant she and Dominique could talk babies. Even Ali had promised to make an appearance, though not for the dinner, just for the auction. He hadn't been going to set his rich Arab foot in the door till Renée showed him the glossy brochure Charmaine had put together that listed all the items to be auctioned and explained where all the money raised would be going.

His change of mind had still surprised everyone at cards last Friday night; Ali kept his public appearances to a minimum because of security reasons. Perhaps the venue sold him on coming. The Regency Hotel had a reputation for keeping its famous and wealthy clientele very safe indeed.

'By the way, I managed to fill my table at last,' she told Charmaine. 'Another of my card-playing friends agreed to come. Did I mention to you I play poker with a high-rolling crowd every Friday night, in the presidential suite at the Regency Hotel no less?'

'No, you've never mentioned that. How interesting. You own racehorses as well, don't you?'

'Yes. Racing is a passion with me, I admit. So is poker. I'm a mad gambler. Anyway, you'll also be

pleased to know that these other mad gamblers I play poker with are all filthy rich. Charles Brandon is one of them. You know, the brewery magnate?'

'Oh, yes, I met him at a recent première party at Fox Studios. He has a stunner of a wife, doesn't he?'

'That's the one. Dominique's her name. They're good for a few grand at the auction. Both have hearts of gold. Can't say quite the same about my number-four poker-playing partner, but he can be generous on occasion. He's—'

'Are you ready to order, ladies?' the waitress interrupted.

'Just give us a moment,' Charmaine said, and the waitress hurried off to attend to another table. The restaurant they were having lunch at was situated on one of the renovated wharves at Wooloomooloo, right on the harbour. Only a stone's throw from the city centre, it was very trendy and very popular, particularly at lunch time on a splendid spring day.

'Enough about the auction, Renée,' Charmaine said firmly. 'Back to the business at hand. *Food.* Shall we be bad and order something fattening for once?' She picked up the menu and started perusing it avidly. 'Gosh, this is all so tempting! It's been months since I had a hamburger. I hear the designer hamburgers here are out of this world. Ooh, and look, there's mango cheesecake on the dessert list. I have a penchant for cheesecake. Damn it, I'm definitely ordering that. With cream,' she finished up defiantly.

Renée laughed. She knew first-hand that models rarely ate anything really fattening, not even the naturally curvy variety like Charmaine. 'You can, if you like,' she said, 'but not me. I've already put on eight

kilos with this pregnancy, and I'm told I could double that if I go full term.'

'Do you know what sex the babies are?' Charmaine asked.

Renée beamed as she always did when asked about her precious twins. 'I do indeed. A boy and a girl. Aren't I just the luckiest woman in the world?'

Till she'd married Rico, Renée had thought she'd never have children. But with her husband's love and support and the best IVF team in Australia, she was now, at the ripe old age of thirty-six, expecting not just one baby, but two! Rico was over the moon and Renée was ecstatic. Everything had gone very well so far and, other than the occasional spot of heartburn and backache, she felt as fit as a fiddle.

Charmaine smiled at her. 'I imagine you just might be. Although my mum is a pretty lucky lady. There again, she's married to my dad, so perhaps I'm biased.'

Renée absorbed this piece of information with some surprise. Charmaine never talked about her family. For some reason, Renée had assumed she was estranged from them these days. Clearly, she was mistaken. Maybe they'd just lost touch a bit. Charmaine's life was a hectic one, what with the demands on her time for her career, and now her charity work.

Renée knew from earlier Press articles about Charmaine that her parents were country folk who ran a cotton farm out west of the Great Divide, pretty well in the middle of nowhere. Their nearest town only had one garage, one hotel and one general store. From the time she was fifteen, Charmaine had used to work behind the counter of that store at the weekend, and during lulls—which was probably most of the time—

filled in her time reading magazines about models and
dreaming of one day being one herself. At fifteen and
a half, she'd entered her photograph into a teen magazine's cover-girl competition, and won. By sixteen
she was strutting her stuff on the catwalk in Sydney
during Australia's fashion week.

Renée had been a model herself back then and recalled how peeved all the other older models were
when this inexperienced teenage upstart carrying far
too many curves had upstaged them. But she'd been
an instant hit, especially with the designers. On
Charmaine's tall yet shapely figure, all clothes looked
fabulous, and so sexy. When Charmaine had to go
home for a while with a nasty case of glandular fever
the other models had breathed a sigh of relief. But
she'd returned to Sydney the following year and taken
up right where she left off.

By then eighteen, a slightly slimmer but more ma-
ture-looking Charmaine had been simply stunning.
Ravishing was how she was described by the fashion
Press. Ravishing and ready to rule the modelling
world. She hadn't quite done that, but she was soon
right up there with the best of them, and Renée's
agency now had a piece of that success.

'Do you take after your mother or your father?'
Renée asked, her curiosity aroused.

'Both, in looks. But neither in character. Mum's a
sweetie and Dad's an old softie. I might act soft and
sweet, but underneath I'm a total bitch,' she said, then
laughed. 'But then, you already know that, don't
you?'

'Not at all,' Renée replied, astounded. 'You play
hardball in business matters but that's not the same.
I've met plenty of total bitches in my life and trust

me, Charmaine, you are certainly not one of them. A total bitch wouldn't work so hard for charity for starters, I can tell you.'

'Aah, but that's my only Achilles heel,' Charmaine said, looking sad and wistful for a moment. 'Kids with cancer. Poor little mites. I can bear it when life is unspeakably cruel and unfair to adults. But not children. They do not deserve that fate. Not when they've done *nothing* to cause it.'

She swallowed, then gritted her teeth.

You're not going to cry, are you? Crying never achieves a thing. Crying is for babies, and the broken-hearted. You're hardly a baby, and your heart isn't broken any more, Charmaine. It's been super-glued back together and nothing will ever break it again.

She reached for the complimentary glass of water that sat on the café table and sipped it till she had herself totally under control. Then she put the glass down and smiled at the woman opposite her, who had a worried frown on her lovely face.

'Sorry,' she said. 'I get emotional when I talk about kids with cancer.'

'There's no need to be sorry. I think what you feel is very admirable. I can understand it entirely.'

Charmaine refrained from laughing at this statement. How could Renée possibly understand? No one could understand who hadn't been through it themselves. Watched a child suffer and die. A sweet, innocent little child.

But she probably meant well.

How old *was* Renée? Charmaine wondered. Early thirties? Older? Must be a bit older, though she still looked marvellous. Some women glowed when they

were pregnant. Others looked drawn and dreary. Renée was clearly the glowing kind.

The waitress materialised at their table again.

'Ready to order yet, ladies?' she asked chirpily.

'Absolutely,' Charmaine replied and ordered the Caribbean-style beef-burger with fries and salad, mango cheesecake with cream, and a cappuccino.

When Renée stared at her, she laughed. 'Don't worry. I won't eat any dinner tonight and I'll punish myself in the gym tomorrow.' As she always did. Every single day.

But then her whole life was now a punishment, wasn't it? For her sins, especially that one really wicked sin, the one she could never forgive herself for, the one she would never forget.

'You'll have to if you hope to fit into that dress you're planning to wear on Saturday night,' Renée pointed out. 'As it is, it looks as if you've been sewn into it.'

'Oh, darn, you're right. I'd momentarily forgotten about that.' She sighed and looked up at the patiently waiting waitress. 'Could I change my order to something less fattening, like a lettuce leaf *au naturel*?'

The waitress grinned. 'I'm so glad you have to watch what you eat, too. If I thought you could look the way you do without suffering even a little, it would kill me.'

'Then do not despair,' Charmaine said drily. 'I suffer more than a little. I suffer a lot every single day.' And then some! 'OK, give me the fish of the day, grilled, with a side salad. No dressing. No dessert. And black coffee to follow. How's that?' she asked Renée.

Renée laughed. 'Perfect. I'll have the same.'

CHAPTER TWO

THE ballroom at the Regency Hotel was a popular Sydney venue for top-drawer functions. Its spectacular Versailles-inspired walls had borne witness to many society balls, awards nights, fashion extravaganzas, product launches, company Christmas parties and, yes, quite a few charity benefits. Its ornate, high-domed ceilings and huge chandeliers had looked down upon the rich and famous on many occasions as they gathered in their finery to celebrate or support whatever cause had brought them together.

Tonight's cause was one which never failed to touch even the most hard-hearted. Kids with cancer. Charmaine knew that for a fact. And she'd exploited it shamelessly as she'd put together this, her first charity banquet and auction.

But it had been one hell of a lot of work, taking up every spare moment of her time for the last six months. Her social life—what there was of it these days—had suffered accordingly. Even her career had suffered, with her refusing any assignments that would take her overseas for more than a few days.

But it was all worth it to see the fantastic turn-out tonight. Every table filled, and all by people who could well afford the hefty thousand-dollar price tag on each ticket. For which they would get a moderately nice sit-down dinner which probably cost less than fifty dollars a head to produce.

Not that the Friends of Kids with Cancer founda-

tion had to pay anything at all for the catering. The relatively new owner of the Regency Hotel had been persuaded to donate the three hundred dinners required, plus all the drinks and the ballroom itself. Charmaine had discovered that Max Richmond's brother had died of cancer when quite a young man, an unfortunate tragedy which she'd been quick to capitalise on.

Ah, yes, there wasn't anything she wouldn't stoop to to raise money to reach tonight's ten-million-dollar target, including going without food of any appreciable kind both yesterday and today so that she could fit into the dress she was wearing as co-host of tonight's auction, a dress that almost defied description.

Wicked was the word that sprang to mind.

How she came to be wearing this particular dress was intriguing. She'd gone to see the head of Campbell Jewels at her home, as she'd personally visited all of the CEOs of Sydney's top companies, begging and bulldozing them for donations for her auction. Most accommodated her in some way. Celeste Campbell had been very amenable, donating a lovely selection of jewellery. She'd also had that no-nonsense, straight-down-the-line manner that Charmaine admired in a woman. Charmaine had warmed to her immediately, and vice versa.

When Celeste found out the charity auction was being held in the Regency ballroom, she'd related to Charmaine the story of another auction that had been held there a decade earlier, not long before Charmaine herself had first come to Sydney. Apparently there'd been a sit-down banquet, like tonight, followed by the auction of the famed black opal called the Heart of Fire, which was now in the Australian Museum.

Charmaine had been startled to learn that during the course of the evening there'd been an attempted robbery *and* a shooting. Charmaine had been fascinated by the woman's story, then totally blown away when Celeste showed her the dress she'd worn that night. It was one of the most provocative evening gowns Charmaine had ever seen.

When Celeste proclaimed she was too old to wear such a dress these days, Charmaine had swiftly jumped in and asked if she could borrow it to wear to the charity auction. She'd known straight away that it was just the thing to get some rich fool to bid a ridiculous price for a dinner date with her. Celeste Campbell had refused—and given her the gown instead! Charmaine had been thrilled.

And now here she was, wearing it, but not feeling quite so confident, or so cocky. Her stomach was doing more somersaults than it had on her very first modelling assignment. Yet she was never nervous these days, no matter how much flesh she was flaunting.

Not that Celeste Campbell's dress showed all that much bare flesh. Its wickedness was far more subtle than that.

There was nothing at all risqué about its basic full-length strapless style, except perhaps that her breasts were having difficulty being confined in the tightly boned bodice, which was two sizes too small for her. Even that little problem was hidden to some degree by the layer of sheer chiffon stretched over the satin underdress, the chiffon reaching high up around the neck and running tightly down her arms to her wrists.

It was the skin tone of both the satin material and the chiffon, plus the selected beading on the front and

back of the gown that was wicked, because it created the illusion of her wearing not a ballgown, but a very skimpy and exotic costume. From even a short distance, the skin-coloured material took on the appearance of bare flesh, with just the shimmering pattern made by the gold beads standing out.

At a glance, front-on, it looked as though the beads were stuck to her nude body in the shape of a bikini. Side-on, where there were no beads, she looked naked. Viewed from the back, the sight was possibly even more provocative, with nothing but skin-coloured chiffon to her waist, a triangular smattering of beads across her behind and a split up the middle back seam to the very top of her thighs. At least the split meant she could walk with her usual long-legged stride instead of tottering around.

Because walk she had to do, right out onto the catwalk that had been put together for the fashion parade conducted earlier during the dinner. The long, well-lit walkway jutted out from the middle of the stage, bisecting the ballroom and giving the occupants of all the tables a top view, especially the ones seated close by. In rehearsal the other night Charmaine had told Rico she would parade out there whilst he auctioned off her dinner-date prize, an idea that hadn't seemed all that bold at the time, possibly because she'd been wearing jeans.

This outrageous dress, however, had sent her usual boldness packing. Charmaine had been bothered by it all evening. Fortunately, during the dinner she hadn't eaten, she'd been sitting down. Seated, the dress was quite modest.

But she was no longer seated. She was up on the ballroom stage, peering through the heavy, wine-

coloured stage curtain at the huge crowd down below and trying to control this alien fear that she was about to make the most shameless display of herself.

What on earth was wrong with her? She wasn't usually like this. Usually, she didn't give a damn how little she wore or if people stared at her, especially the men.

A scornful anger quickly replaced these highly uncharacteristic qualms. Let them think what they liked. She really didn't care as long as one of them coughed up with a big fat cheque for her foundation.

Feeling marginally better, she glanced at her slender gold wrist-watch and was thinking it was high time for Rico to make an appearance to begin the auction when a very male whistle split the air behind her. She whirled and the man himself was standing there, smiling a wry smile.

'That is *some* dress, Charmaine. Are you sure you won't be arrested for wearing it?'

'I've worn less,' she retorted, nervous tension making her snappy.

'Yes, but in this case more is worse.'

'Do try not to leer, Rico.'

'I never leer.'

'No,' she conceded with a sigh. 'No, you don't. Sorry. Actually, you're much nicer than I thought you'd be, for someone who's so darned good-looking.' Which he was. Tall, dark and handsome. But not the kind of tall, dark and handsome that she'd once found irresistible. Big and macho were not her preference. She'd always preferred the leaner, more elegant kind of man.

'Thank you,' Rico replied. 'I think.' Straightening

his bow-tie, he scooped in a deep breath. 'So! Shall we get this show on the road?'

Again, nerves rushed in, making her want to turn tail and run. Which in turn brought forth a redeeming rush of defiance. 'Too right,' she said. 'It's time to make those poor kids some serious bucks.'

'Amen to that!' Rico agreed.

The auction started off well, at that point the target of ten million looking within easy reach. But the economic times were tough and around halfway the bids began to lag. No matter how much Rico cajoled, by the time the auction had only two prizes left, the amount raised was just under seven million. Charmaine sighed her disappointment. The island holiday Rico was about to offer might make fifty grand. But that would still leave a shortfall of nearly three million. Even if she went out onto the catwalk stark naked, no man here was going to bid that much just to have dinner with her.

'We're not even going to make *seven* million,' she groaned after Rico sold the holiday for a paltry thirty thousand.

'No, it doesn't look like it,' Rico replied quietly, having placed his hands over the microphone. 'Perhaps you should have got yourself a real auctioneer.'

'Don't be ridiculous. You've been marvellous. It's not you. It's the times. People are getting tight. We've really done quite well. My hopes were too high. Come on, let's see what we can get for my pathetic prize.'

'Now who's being ridiculous? A dinner date with you is anything but a pathetic prize, Charmaine.'

'Flatterer. Just get on with it. I want to get this

torment over and done with.' A telling comment, but true. She'd never felt this reluctant to sell herself.

'Now, ladies and gentlemen, on to the last prize of the evening,' Rico began again, reviving that Italian accent which seemed to come and go at will. 'Our lovely hostess, Charmaine, one of Australia's top supermodels, is offering a dinner date with herself right here in the Regency's own fabulous By Candlelight restaurant, to be taken next Saturday night. This is a fabulous prize to end this evening with and one which I'm sure will command a top offer.'

He flashed Charmaine an encouraging smile then muttered, 'Off you go, sweetheart,' under his breath. 'Strut your stuff.'

Charmaine rolled her eyes at him, but off she went, undulating her way down the catwalk, doing her best to smile through gritted teeth, well aware that all eyes in that ballroom were glued to her body. Not that *she* could see much. The footlights that bathed her in light threw the rest of the ballroom into relative darkness. She could see silhouetted shapes but no details, no actual eyes.

Yet she could feel them stripping her in a way that she had never felt before. It had to be because of this darned dress. What else *could* it be?

'Might I remind you that Charmaine was recently voted the sexiest woman in Australia by a national magazine?' Rico raved on. 'You can see for yourself that that tag is no exaggeration. I would imagine having a private dinner with such a stunning creature would be some man's dream come true. So come along, gentlemen, make your bids for this once-in-a-lifetime privilege!'

Charmaine almost winced with embarrassment.

Dear heavens, now she felt as though she was on the auction block of some white slaver, and that it was her body being sold, not just a few hours of her companionship.

But what the heck, she reminded herself, if the foundation ended up with a good wad of money? Still, she thanked the lord that she'd banned the Press from this do. The last thing she could stand at this moment would be being besieged with camera flashes, not to mention the prospect of seeing photographs of herself in this dress splashed all across the Sunday papers tomorrow morning, accompanied by some trashy story.

With the comfort of that last thought, she plastered a more sultry smile on her face and sashayed sexily down to the end of the catwalk, where she stood motionless for a few moments, her hands on her hips in a saucy attitude. Then slowly, seductively, she turned, the audience gasping at the sight of her back view.

Her eyes connected with Rico's and he grinned a rather lascivious grin. 'Don't be coy, now,' he urged the audience. 'If I were a single man myself, I would put my hat in the ring, I can tell you. But I'm out of the market, as my lovely wife right there will attest.'

He nodded down towards a table on Charmaine's immediate left. She automatically glanced down, then froze.

Later that night, long after this ghastly moment was well behind her, Charmaine would be grateful she hadn't been moving at the time, for she would surely have stumbled. Maybe even fallen. As it was, she still felt as if the floor had opened up under her.

At least now she knew why she'd been feeling so

aware of male eyes on her. Because *this* pair of eyes had been hiding amongst the others.

Dark, beautiful eyes. Hard eyes. Dangerous eyes.

Prince Ali of Dubar, sitting right there at Renée's table, looking dashing and debonair in a black dinner suit and gazing up at her with a coolly arrogant air.

Shock galvanised Charmaine's brain as well as her body, several blank moments passing before she regained her composure and could even *try* to put two and two together. What on earth was this man doing sitting at Renée's table? Surely they couldn't be *friends*!

This unlikely possibility had barely surfaced before things which had seemed unimportant or irrelevant at the time flashed back into her mind. The prince himself, mentioning last year that he spent every weekend in Sydney going to the races and playing cards with friends. And then Renée the other day at lunch, talking about the high-rollers she played poker with every Friday night in this very hotel, in one of the presidential suites.

Who else could afford a presidential suite but a president, or a rock-star, or an oil-rich sheikh? The worst possible scenario of that little trio, of course, was the sheikh, especially one whom she'd derided and belittled and rejected and who was here tonight for one thing and one thing only. To make her eat her words that she would never go to dinner with a man like him.

Prince Ali of Dubar was undoubtedly going to be the highest bidder for the dinner date with her. Why else would he have come? He hadn't bid for anything else so far tonight. She would have noticed if he had, a spotlight always briefly being shone on the suc-

cessful bidder after an item was knocked down to them.

No, it would not be some total stranger sitting opposite her at dinner next Saturday night. It would be this man, whose pride she had severely dented last year. Now it was his turn to humiliate her, by forcing her to dine with him for several hours and endure not only his company, but also his none-too-subtle coveting of her body.

The impact of this realisation sent bile rising in Charmaine's throat. Pride demanded she would not submit herself to such a mortifying situation. But pride also demanded she conduct herself with her usual self-contained, I'm-not-afraid-of-anything-or-any-man demeanour. After all, even if the sheikh was the successful bidder—and every cell in her brain shouted to her that he would be—what could he really do to her in a public restaurant, across the table? Proposition her once more? Try to seduce her with his charm?

This last idea was laughable.

No. Let him have his pathetic little moment of triumph.

Quite deliberately, she smiled straight at him, challenging him boldly with her eyes and her mouth.

Come on, sucker. Make your bid. See if I care.

His dark eyes narrowed a little at her smile, then slowly raked over her from head to toe, as though assessing if she was worth bidding for. For a split-second, Charmaine worried that he might *not* bid. Maybe he'd come to dent her pride *that* way.

But even as she was besieged by a thousand ambivalent emotions over this possibility, his royal mouth opened.

'Five million dollars,' he said firmly, and she gasped. She couldn't help it. Neither could the rest of the people there.

Even Rico sucked in sharply. 'Wow! That is some bid. Ladies and gentlemen, Prince Ali of Dubar has bid five million dollars for the privilege of a dinner date with our lovely Charmaine. Somehow, I don't think there will be any better offers, but if there is some intrepid gentleman out there willing to top his royal highness's offer, will he speak up now or forever hold his peace?'

Charmaine winced at Rico's words, which were reminiscent of a wedding ceremony. Rather ironic, given this was as far from a romantic encounter as one could get. His royal highness just wanted the opportunity to make her eat humble pie, and he was willing to spend an exorbitant amount of money to do so.

'No more offers? In that case...*sold* to His Royal Highness, Prince Ali of Dubar!' Rico brought the gavel down on the rostrum with a loud thump that reverberated right through Charmaine.

Everyone in the ballroom started clapping, more so when the red arrow on the huge target metre displayed at the side of the stage was lifted by its attendant to twelve million dollars. Charmaine was forced to keep smiling when in fact she'd rather have been screaming, preferably at the man whose black eyes remained locked onto hers, his superior air evoking in her a burning desire to tell him that no man would *ever* own even a small piece of her, not even her time!

But, of course, that wish was to remain unrequited. No way could she turn down a five-million-dollar windfall for a cause that meant more than her silly

pride. On top of that, no way in the wide world would Charmaine let this arrogant devil see how rattled and angry she was. To show anger was to show she cared. She resolved then and there to remain impeccably polite to him next Saturday night. There would be no further outbursts of temper. No rude remarks. No attempts to cut him down to size.

Given this was her intention, she really could not afford to stay standing where she was any longer. The way he kept looking at her was not conducive to ongoing politeness.

Lord knows how I'm going to control myself when I'm alone with him, Charmaine worried as she made her way—to further clapping—off the catwalk.

'I still can't believe it,' Rico said to her after he'd wrapped up the auction and clicked off the microphone. 'Good old Ali, bidding five mil just to have dinner with you. The man must have more money than sense. No offence meant, Charmaine. But even you must agree that was over-the-top.'

Charmaine frowned at Rico's familiar remarks before realising that of course *he* had to be well acquainted with the prince as well, not just Renée.

'You sound as if you're really old friends,' came her careful comment. As much as she despised herself for it, she couldn't help being curious about the man who'd just paid five million dollars to have dinner with her.

'We are,' Rico admitted. 'Been playing cards together every Friday night for nearly six years now. Been partners in a few racehorses over the years as well. Ali's a great bloke. You'll like him.'

Charmaine's top lip curled before she could stop it. But then she decided not to be a total hypocrite. There

was only so far she was prepared to carry pretence, and in private was not one of them.

'The prince and I have met once before,' she confessed curtly. 'I didn't like him then and I don't like him now.'

Rico looked startled. 'You've met before? Where?'

'At the Melbourne Cup carnival last year. I was one of the fashion judges there on Ladies' Day. To put it bluntly, your royal friend hit on me.'

'*And?*'

'What do you mean, *and*? And *nothing*! I told you. I didn't like him.'

'That surprises me. Women usually do.'

'Maybe that's why I didn't like him,' she snapped. 'Look, it's immaterial whether I like him or not. He's bought my company over dinner for a few hours and I'll honour that. But if you're talking to your Arab friend, then I suggest you warn him that paying five million dollars gives him no more privileges—or rights—than he had by paying for my lunch the last time. Yes, tell him that, Rico. Oh, and tell him I will be at the By Candlelight restaurant promptly at seven next Saturday night, but he is not to attempt to contact me before that. I would be very annoyed if my private and unlisted phone number somehow found its way into his royal highness's hands. *Comprenez-vous?*'

'I get the picture. I just wonder if you do.'

'Meaning?'

'Meaning Ali is not given to flights of fancy. After what you've just told me, I suspect he came here to-night specifically to bid for that dinner with you, money being no object. Which leads me to believe that he must be somewhat smitten with you. If so,

then I doubt your supposed disliking him at first sight will prove to be any more than a minor hurdle.'

Charmaine bristled. 'Is that some kind of warning?'

'I suppose so. Look, if you really don't like him, then watch yourself. Ali is not a man to be toyed with.'

'I have *never* toyed with him.'

'Come, now, Charmaine. I saw the way you were smiling down at him just now and that was not the smile of an uninterested woman.'

Heat zoomed into Charmaine's cheeks. 'You don't understand. I was just…just…'

'Taunting him?'

She shrugged irritably. 'In a way.'

'Don't,' came his sharp rebuke. 'That's not the way to behave with a man like Ali. Such behaviour could make him…dangerous.'

Her eyes widened. '*Dangerous?* In what way?'

Rico shook his head. 'Look, I'll speak to him. Make sure he understands how the land lies. I'm sure he'll respect your wishes if he believes you're genuinely not interested. You are definitely not interested?'

'Oh, please. Spare me from having to deal with a spoiled sheikh who harbours Hollywood fantasies over his irresistibility to women.'

'Maybe he has cause to harbour them.'

She could not contain a scornful laugh. 'The only thing Prince Ali of Dubar has going for him with me is the size of his wallet. And then only if he opens it for the foundation. You tell him that, Rico. Now I really must go and take off this infernal dress!'

A famous saying came to Rico's mind as he watched Charmaine flounce off, her glamorous drop

earrings swinging sexily around her shoulders and her long fair hair swishing back and forth across her nearly naked back.

'The lady doth protest too much, methinks.'

CHAPTER THREE

SHORTLY before six on the following Saturday afternoon, Charmaine climbed out from behind the wheel of her nondescript white sedan, collected her overnight bag from the back seat, handed the car keys to the valet parking attendant and proceeded into the arcade-style foyer of the Regency Hotel, all without having to tolerate the harassing presence of the paparazzi.

Experience had taught the supermodel several ways to avoid them. If possible, she arrived early for publicised events, often in disguise. Unfortunately, her dinner date tonight with the sheikh was now a well-publicised event, courtesy of one pesky female journalist who'd been at the auction and written it up the following day, the main focus of her article being the astonishing amount paid by Prince Ali of Dubar for a dinner date with *our* Charmaine. Typically, the find-a-sexual-angle journo made it all sound impossibly romantic.

Charmaine had quickly regretted announcing at the auction when and where the dinner would take place. That had been a mistake. But no way was she going to contact the prince and change the arrangements. She did, however, contact the owner of the Regency again and was assured by Mr Richmond that no Press would bother either her or his most esteemed guest from Dubar over dinner. He promised heightened se-

curity at both the hotel entrance and complete privacy in the restaurant.

Charmaine expressed her gratitude but still booked a room in the hotel so that she could arrive early and dress there, as well as stay the night. That way she could slip out the following morning in her own good time.

Now here she was, blessedly anonymous as she walked up to the reception desk in her nondescript brown wig and wraparound sunglasses, not having had to tolerate cameras being shoved in her face and having questions shouted at her. What a relief! She might have lost her cool if there'd been reporters and photographers hanging around the hotel. It had been a very long week and her nerves were on a knife-edge today.

Charmaine glanced at her watch as she rode the lift up to the second floor. Less than an hour to go. But time enough for her to get ready. She'd washed and blow-dried her hair earlier that afternoon. *And* done her nails. All she had left to do was change her clothes and put on some make-up and earrings. None of those preparations would take much time. Charmaine had decided to dress down for this occasion.

If the sheikh thought she'd show up in something reminiscent of last Saturday night then he was in for a surprise. There would be no flesh on show tonight. Nothing for those predatory eyes to feast upon.

At precisely five minutes to seven, she was again in the lift, her stone-washed jeans now replaced by loose-fitting black crêpe evening trousers and a bronze silk Chinese-style tunic top that skimmed her figure and minimised its hourglass curves. Her hair

was brushed straight back from her face and fell in a dead straight curtain to her waist. Her face had hardly any make-up at all. Just a fine layer of foundation, a touch of blue eyeshadow, a few strokes of mascara and some shiny bronze lipstick that matched the colour of her nails. Small diamond studs winked at her ear-lobes, in marked contrast to the sexy shoulder-length drops she'd worn for the auction.

The irony was that with a natural beauty like Charmaine, often less was more. But she was unaware of this fact. Being used to wearing much more make-up, especially for photo shoots and her work on the catwalk, she thought she looked as plain as she could. If only she knew how breathtakingly beautiful—and intriguingly innocent—she looked as she emerged on the mezzanine floor and made her way down the marble-floored corridor to the By Candlelight restaurant.

The *maître d'*, a tall bald-headed man with a thin moustache and intelligent grey eyes, smiled at her from behind his podium-style station.

'Mademoiselle Charmaine,' he said with a French accent, which might or might not have been genuine. The number of *maître d'*s in Sydney restaurants with French accents seemed excessive in Charmaine's opinion. 'Such a delight to have you in our restaurant tonight. His highness has already arrived. I will take you straight to him.'

Charmaine dutifully followed in his wake as he made his way past the mostly empty tables towards the back of the restaurant. Considering the relatively early hour of their 'date', Charmaine was surprised that the prince had already arrived. She would have thought that royalty would always be a little late for engagements of the social kind.

But of course this wasn't a social occasion, she reminded herself ruefully. It was one of vengeance. Naturally, his royal highness wouldn't want to miss a moment of her humiliation.

This last realisation rescued her from any inner resentment at being here at all and sent a small smile playing around her lips. If the sheikh thought he could belittle her tonight, then he was in for more than one surprise. He had no idea what he was dealing with. No idea at all!

The alcove she was taken to was totally and utterly private, a small square-shaped room tucked away in a discreet corner. There was an open archway leading into it, but even this was flanked by huge potted palms that added to its sense of privacy. The walls of the alcove—and even the ceiling—were painted black, the darkness only minimally alleviated by several low-voltage recessed lights. There was no furniture except for the table, which was round and intimately sized, and covered with the same white linen tablecloth as the tables she'd just passed. The wine-coloured candle that graced the glass centrepiece on the table was low, perhaps because the people who normally sought to eat here wanted nothing to spoil their view of each other's face and eyes.

This area had undoubtedly been designed with lovers in mind, a real love-nest for those who wanted to keep prying eyes away whilst they banqueted on the best food and wine and whispered sweet nothings to each other. Tycoons would dine here with their mistresses, and celebrities with their latest live-in lovers.

Charmaine doubted this table would have borne witness to too many dinners like the one that would be served on its elegance surface tonight. Though

possibly it was the *diners* more than the dinner who would be different.

When she'd first walked towards the dimly lit alcove, Charmaine could hardly see the sheikh sitting on the far side of the table, his dark clothes and dark colouring making him melt into the black-walled background. But, once she had passed under the archway and her eyes grew accustomed to the dimmer light, he emerged from the shadow, first his face, and then the rest of him.

Still no traditional Arab dress for him, she noted. He looked like a typical Western playboy, dressed expensively but rather casually in an exquisite black lounge suit and a black silk collarless shirt.

Did her heart beat a little faster at the sight of his handsome elegance? Or was her adrenalin surge simply the result of their next face-to-face confrontation finally being at hand?

Soldiers on the verge of going into battle would feel like this, she reasoned. There would always be a type of excitement alongside the fear.

Fear? Now, that was an odd thought. She had nothing to *fear* from this man.

Or did she?

Rico had said something about his being dangerous. And Rico was no fool. What kind of danger was he talking about? OK, so her date tonight was an Arab sheikh with perhaps more primitive ways in treating women he fancied than most men of the Western world. And yes, he still fancied her, despite what she was wearing tonight. His eyes were like hot coals on her face and body.

So much for her dressing down for the occasion, came the irritable thought. If anything, he seemed to

desire her even more without her curves being on display.

But surely, that was all he could realistically do. *Desire* her. As private as this alcove was, it was hardly conducive to his ravishing her during tonight's dinner date, especially without her consent. One little scream and people would come running.

No, she had nothing to fear about this evening, except her own silly behaviour. Just keep your temper, she lectured herself. And your cool. Then, in three hours' time, you can leave and never see this infernal man ever again.

His rising from his chair as she approached the table startled her. She hadn't expected such a gentlemanly gesture from him.

'Good evening, Charmaine,' he said with a slight nod of his head of perfectly groomed black hair. Quite wavy on top, it was. And thick and clean and shining. The kind of hair that would be a joy to touch.

Charmaine was taken aback by this most alien thought. She never found joy any more in touching any part of any man. And here she was, thinking about running her fingers through *this* man's hair. The very idea!

'You look…lovely,' he added, that dark, desire-filled gaze of his never leaving her face.

Charmaine was grateful that the *maître d'* chose that moment to pull out her chair so she could occupy herself sitting down rather than answering the sheikh. He sat down also, but his eyes stayed glued to her with merciless intent.

The *maître d'* made a production of picking up her linen serviette, shaking it out of its creative folds then

placing it across her lap before making his way round the table and doing the same for the sheikh.

'Your personal waiter for this evening will be along shortly, Your Highness,' he said with a deferential bow towards the prince before hurrying off, leaving them temporarily alone.

For the life of her, Charmaine could not think of a thing to say. She was still rattled by wanting to touch the sheikh's hair. A few seconds of awkward silence ticked away and she longed for their waiter to appear.

Fortunately, he did, a slim, tanned young man with graceful hands and no French accent. He handed them both a menu, ran through the chef's specials of the night, then asked them if they would like to order a pre-dinner drink, or possibly a bottle of wine from the wine list, which he placed beside the sheikh's right elbow.

'Bring me mineral water,' the prince ordered after the briefest of glances. 'Sparkling. I do not drink alcohol of any kind,' he added, for her benefit, it seemed. 'But I do not expect you to follow suit. Please...order anything that you like.' And he handed her the wine list across the table.

'I don't drink alcohol, either,' she replied, and handed it back to the waiter. 'So fizzy water would be fine for me, too.' Whereupon she threw a sweet smile over at her nemesis, satisfied that she'd just sunk any plans he had to get her sloshed and have his wicked way with her in the presidential suite afterwards.

The waiter hurried off to do their bidding, leaving them alone again.

'You never drink alcohol?' the prince asked, sounding more curious than disappointed.

'No.'

'Why is that?'

'Oh, many reasons,' she replied in an airy fashion.

He smiled a wry smile that softened the harsh lines of his mouth. 'Which you don't intend to tell me.'

'How perceptive of you.' She maintained a lightness in her voice but in her lap her hands gripped her serviette as a drowning man would a life-jacket. This man assuredly brought out the worst in her. It was definitely because of the way he looked at her. So...covetously. And at the same time so damned confidently, as though he was already picturing her in his bed. How she would have loved an excuse to slap his supercilious face, to see that polished teak cheek of his glow red with the mark of her handprint.

'You are resenting being here with me tonight.'

It was an effort not to show surprise over his being able to read her so well. Though perhaps his very correct conclusion was not evidence of any great insight on his part. It wouldn't take much brains to realise she'd be far from happy at the situation she found herself in.

'Not at all,' she said, forcing a patently false smile through her clenched jaw. 'My foundation is five million dollars richer because of tonight. How can I possibly resent that?'

'The last time we met, you vowed you'd never have dinner with me,' he reminded her, his eyes watchful.

Her shrug was supremely indifferent. 'That was then and this is now. I discovered long ago that life can throw you some unexpected curves; I find that it's far better to go with the flow rather than fight them.'

His drily amused smile annoyed her. Because she could not read its meaning.

'You are perfectly correct there, my dear Charmaine. Do you mind my calling you Charmaine? No one seemed to know your second name so I don't know what else to call you.'

'Charmaine is fine.'

She was tempted to add that he could leave out the 'my dear' bit, but she knew if she started being persnickety, she would never stop.

'You must call me Ali,' he pronounced.

Now, *that* was expecting too much. 'I don't think so, Your Highness,' she said crisply. 'That is far too intimate an address. *Everyone* calls me Charmaine, whereas I am sure not everyone calls you Ali. Probably only your relatives and your closest of friends, of which I am neither.'

His eyes blazed momentarily, giving her a glimpse of what Rico had meant by his being dangerous. The man had a right royal temper when crossed. But then, so did she.

'Why are you so determined to be rude to me?' he demanded to know.

'Actually, I am determined to be anything *but* rude this evening,' she countered. 'Sometimes, we Australians are mistakenly thought of as rude when in fact we are just trying to be honest. Calling a spade a spade, so to speak. You bought a dinner date with me tonight, Your Highness. You did not buy anything else. I told Rico to make that perfectly clear to you this week. Did he forget to relay my message?'

'No. Enrico told me exactly what you said. And I took careful note. Perhaps it was foolish of me but I hoped you might be persuaded to put aside your ir-

rational dislike. I was looking forward to the opportunity to show you that I am not… What was it you called me last year? A spoiled and arrogant man who had not had no said to him often enough?'

'That sounds about right,' she replied whilst thinking that it was *exactly* what she'd flung at him that day. Clearly, each insulting word had bitten deep into the prince's ego and he meant to exact retribution. All that bulldust about his hoping to show her he was really a good bloke was just that. Bulldust! The only reason she was here tonight was because he *was* spoiled and arrogant, and would *not* take no for an answer.

The waiter arrived with their mineral water, at the same time enquiring if they wanted to order their meals yet. The prince peremptorily waved him away, saying they had not had time to study the menu and not to return for a good ten minutes.

The prospect of ten more minutes of this kind of banter threatened Charmaine's resolve to remain icily polite, so she swept up the menu and used it as a barrier between them.

But blocking that smouldering gaze did not block the memory of it, or the way it made her feel. As if she was a specimen under a microscope.

Charmaine tried to focus on the food on offer, but it was a futile activity. Her mind had other ideas, giving rise to a fanciful image of herself as a beautiful and rare butterfly, with the prince an obsessed collector of beautiful and rare butterflies.

In her mind's eye, she could see him sitting at a table in a lush garden somewhere and watching her flit from flower to flower. Watching and waiting, oh, so patiently. She did not see the net he had hidden

by his chair and when she foolishly flew too close he struck, and suddenly she was captured, unable to escape her fate—which was to be his, either dead or alive.

Charmaine came back to reality with a jolt, her heartbeat racing with alarm. Yet that was crazy, to be alarmed by a daydream, a fanciful concoction of her own imagination. And yet alarm was exactly what she was suddenly feeling.

Tightening her grip on the rather large leatherbound menu, she lowered it slowly, only to find those eyes still watching her as she'd imagined the butterfly collector had watched the butterfly.

The panic that rose in her chest made her angry.

'I have no idea what to order,' she said brusquely, and snapped the menu shut. 'Would you mind choosing something for me, Your Highness? I'm not a fussy eater so you can't really go wrong. I eat almost anything. Except prunes. I hate prunes.'

'You don't drink and you eat almost anything. A most unusual Western woman,' he muttered, but at least his eyes dropped to the menu, and away from her.

The release in tension this afforded Charmaine was amazing. She actually sighed with it and leant back into her chair.

'You sound tired,' he remarked, but thankfully without looking up.

'I've had a very busy week.'

'With your charity work, or modelling?' he asked, again without looking up.

'I've been doing a lengthy photo shoot for the Femme Fatale company. People think that being a model is glamorous work, but it's really very ex-

hausting, getting dressed and undressed all the time and being prodded and pushed into a hundred different poses.' How much easier it was to chat away whilst those unsettling eyes were occupied elsewhere. 'Still, I suppose I shouldn't complain. At least with Femme Fatale, I get to keep all the lovely lingerie used in the shoot.'

Now those incredible eyes rose again, and once again she felt as firmly pinned as any poor butterfly on a collector's wall.

Charmaine had to concede that she'd never come across eyes so powerful, or so wickedly hypnotic. She would imagine that a normal woman would find it difficult not to fall under their spell.

Just as well she wasn't normal, then. Or the sheikh might have succeeded in his intention to seduce her. Because of course that was part of his plan tonight. Seduction. His pride wanted more from her than her company over one miserable dinner. He wanted *her* pride. He wanted her naked and willing in his bed.

Such imagery produced an almost hysterical amusement that reduced this infernal tension gripping her insides, and restored her earlier dry humour over this situation. Poor Prince Ali. He really had set his sights on a lemon this time.

'I didn't realise Femme Fatale sold lingerie,' he commented thoughtfully. 'I thought they were a perfume company. That was where I first saw you, playing Salome in one of their television advertisements.'

So that was what had first sparked his sexual interest! Charmaine wasn't surprised. The costume she'd worn as the biblical namesake of Femme Fatale's latest perfume was provocative to say the

least. So was her dance of the seven veils—although for television censorship she'd had to stop at five.

'Femme Fatale has become well-known because of their highly successful perfume range, it's true,' she advised him. 'But they started out in lingerie. Very sexy lingerie,' she added naughtily. 'I'm the face of their summer range, which will shortly be advertised on their mail-order website.'

His nostrils flared. So did his eyes. 'You are to be on the internet, half-naked, for all the world to see?'

His reaction both amused and annoyed her. 'I will be by the end of next week. You look shocked, Your Highness. I suppose you think it immoral for me to be photographed wearing underwear and nightwear.'

The muscles in his jaw flexed several times, as though he was struggling with his emotions. 'I think it...beneath you.'

'Indeed! Well, that's your prerogative. It's a free country. Unlike your own, I imagine. At least where your women are concerned. I'm sure the men in Dubar have all the freedom in the world to do and think whatever they like, whilst the women are confined and controlled.'

His eyes narrowed till they were two angry slits burning under his straight black brows. 'Please do not betray your ignorance of my country, *and* my culture. Women in Dubar are respected and protected, not confined and controlled.'

Charmaine would have loved to argue with him further but the return of their waiter for their meal order brought a perhaps fortuitous halt to that topic. Her blood was getting hot, a danger signal if she meant to keep her cool. After all, the evening was still very young.

So she sat there prudently silent whilst the prince ordered all three courses of their meal in a rather abrupt tone. An oriental prawn dish as entrée. Crispy roast duckling for the main. And a decadent-sounding chocolate concoction for dessert.

Charmaine suppressed a sigh over the number of calories she would down tonight. Stress always made her hungry and tonight was proving exceptionally stressful, despite her feeling reasonably satisfied with her performance so far. Still, such sinful oral decadence would mean an added hour in the gym tomorrow.

But no matter. She had nothing else to do. There were no boyfriends in her life any more to demand her spare weekend hours. Her fund-raising work had ended for the year, thanks to his royal highness's contribution, and she had no modelling assignments tomorrow.

Sunday was not a day usually chosen for fashion parades, and rarely for photographic work. Too many people around to spoil the shoot, which often as not was done outdoors these days. She also wasn't required to fly off anywhere. Thank the lord. In fact, she had nothing coming up for a fortnight, after which she was booked solid till Christmas, with an overseas shoot in Italy for next year's Pirelli calendar. Then it was back to Melbourne for Australia's fashion week.

She really should take advantage of the next fortnight and rest. She could go visit her parents, she supposed. She hadn't seen them for ages. But her chest tightened at the thought of going home, so Charmaine decided to leave any visiting till Christmas, when it could not be avoided.

'I presume,' the prince began as soon as the waiter

departed, 'that there is nothing I can say to change your mind about the kind of man I am. You have already prejudged me because I am an Arab. You have condemned me without a hearing because of my country and my culture.'

Charmaine took a few calming sips of her mineral water before answering. 'Your being an Arab has little to do with my feelings, or *non*-feelings for you, Your Highness. Although I have to confess that I'm not impressed with the way women are treated like second-class citizens in your world. You can deny it but your history speaks for itself. And so, increasingly, are some of your women, the brave ones who risk all to speak up for themselves. What riles me about men like you, however, is not so much your country or your culture but your obscene wealth and your arrogant presumptions. Billionaires believe their money can buy them anything they desire. Planes. Palaces. Racehorses. *Me*.'

He said nothing for a moment or two. But then he leant back in his chair, removing his face from the circle of light thrown by the candle, his expressive eyes now hidden in shadow.

'You think I just *desire* you?' came his quietly delivered question.

She bristled at this ridiculous attempt to deny that his interest in her was strictly sexual. 'I *know* you just desire me, Your Highness. You made me brutally aware of your lust from the first moment we met. You watched me all that day at the races, then presumptuously expected me to say yes to whatever your royal self wanted. It knocked you for six when I turned your dinner invitation down, so much so that when you got the chance you paid five million dollars to force me

to do what I told you I would never do willingly. So yes, I think you were being excessively optimistic tonight to hope that I would put aside my very *rational* dislike of you. And no, there is nothing you can say or do to make me change my mind about what kind of man you are. I already know what kind you are. I've met your kind before.'

'Oh, I doubt that, dear lady,' he said in a tone that sent shivers running up and down her spine. When he came forward again, back into the light, his face was hard and handsome and ominously determined. 'In that case,' he ground out, 'you leave me no alternative.'

Charmaine swallowed. 'What do you mean? No alternative…?'

A prickling sensation ran over her skin, breaking it out into goosebumps. Whatever he was about to say, Charmaine knew she wasn't going to like it.

'I paid five million dollars for a few short hours of your company here tonight. I will donate five *hundred* million dollars to your precious foundation…if you spend a week with me.'

CHAPTER FOUR

CHARMAINE gaped at him.

'You can't be serious!'

'I am deadly serious.'

Charmaine's hand shook as she lifted her mineral water to her lips, taking several reviving sips before she placed the glass back on the table. 'You must be mad,' she muttered.

'Possibly. But that is beside the point. The offer is genuine. What is your answer?'

Her mouth opened to tell him no. Never in a million years. But somehow the words didn't find her tongue. The sum of five hundred million dollars kept rolling round and round in her head. Five...*hundred*...million...dollars. Half a billion. An absolute fortune!

Charmaine could not hope to raise that amount in a lifetime of modelling and fund-raising. Yet it would be all hers to do immense good with...if she spent one short week in the sheikh's bed.

No use pretending he just wanted her company. The name of the game was sex this time.

'One week, you said?' she asked, and knew she'd taken her first step on the slippery slide to hell.

When his eyes glittered with a dark triumph she wanted to snatch back those telling words. But she did not. And the deal was already halfway to being sealed.

'Actually, not even a week,' he went on oh, so

coolly. 'I leave here by helicopter to return to my property every Sunday evening around six, and arrive back in Sydney each Friday afternoon around the same time. So it's really only five days. That represents one hundred million dollars a day for your time.'

'My *time*!' she scoffed. 'Now, that's one hell of an understatement. You want a lot more from me than my time, Your Highness. You want me to sleep with you.'

He did not deny a thing, his eyes remaining fixed on hers as she battled all sorts of inner demons.

'I would want the money up front,' she demanded, even as her mind reeled at the thought of actually going to bed with this man, of being at his sexual beck and call for five days and five nights.

Yet on the surface she betrayed nothing, her own gaze not wavering from his face, her own cool matching his. Was that her pride doing that? Or just practice? She'd long perfected the art of not letting any man think he'd got the better of her.

'Naturally,' he agreed. 'If you say yes, the full amount will be transferred into your foundation's account on Monday. For which I will expect you to present yourself—suitably packed—at my hotel suite on the following Sunday, no later than five o'clock.'

Next Sunday. Eight days away. Eight days to think about what she had to do with him.

'What do you mean by suitably packed?'

'You will need to bring clothes for a wide range of activities.'

Really? she thought drily. She would have thought all she'd need to bring was her birthday suit.

'Such as?'

'There is a heated pool on my property. And a tennis court. And a fully equipped gymnasium, not to mention an unparalleled stable of riding horses. Do you ride?'

'I can stay on. If the horse I'm riding isn't too wild, that is,' she added.

'I will choose a gentle mount for you,' he promised whilst the excited gleam in his eyes suggested her words had prompted thoughts of another kind of riding, and a less than gentle mount. Namely himself.

'You do that,' she snapped, her stomach twisting at the image of herself sitting astride his dark, lean body. 'What's wrong with tomorrow instead of next Sunday?' she added abruptly, deciding that if she was going to do this, then the sooner the better, a bit like getting a tooth out. Any delay would be sheer torture.

He looked startled by her suggestion. 'The money would not be in your foundation's account by then.'

'I could take your word that it would be transferred first thing on the Monday.'

'My word as an Arab?' he retorted mockingly.

'No. Your word as a gentleman. You *are* a gentleman, I hope. If not, then I would not even consider this…arrangement.' Even as she said the words, she realised how laughable they were. Would a gentleman do this—use his obscene wealth to bribe her into his bed?

His smile was wry. 'Please do not try to play me for a fool, Charmaine. You and I both know I am not a gentleman. But I have my own code of honour and I *am* a man of my word. We have mutual friends in Rico and Renée. I am sure they would both vouch for my character.'

She refrained from telling the sheikh that Rico had

actually warned her about him. Pity she'd chosen to ignore that warning.

But how could she possibly have known that he would go to such extreme limits to force her to say yes to him?

Once again, she shivered inside at what was ahead of her. How could she bear to go to bed with him? Just the thought of taking all her clothes off in front of him was making her heart thud and her stomach churn. Yet she'd posed nearly naked lots of times. Paraded herself shamelessly on the catwalk for almost a decade. Stripped down to G-strings in dressing-rooms in front of strangers without batting an eyelid.

So the undressing part shouldn't bother her unduly. Charmaine was not ashamed of her body. Or shy. She supposed it was what was to come *after* the undressing that was perturbing her.

Just think of the money, she told herself sternly. And the enormous good you can do with it. Fund research. Buy expensive medical equipment. Build new hospital wings and homes-away-from-home for families who want to be by their sick children's bedsides and can't afford expensive stays in city hotels.

Such thinking tightened her resolve to do this, no matter what the cost to her pride. She told herself that in a strictly pragmatic sense, going to bed with the sheikh should be no big deal. If he'd been revoltingly fat or ugly or crude it might have been. But he was none of these things. As she'd already noted several times, he was incredibly handsome with a fit, lean body and a graceful and elegant manner. Nothing there to repulse her.

Really, if she could only forget who he was, then it wouldn't be much different from all her other sex-

ual encounters over the years, the ones she'd willingly endured in her futile search for normality. She hadn't enjoyed those other occasions either. Not one little bit. Of course, she had *liked* those men. That was where the difference lay, she supposed. Hard to pretend this man was similar to them. He was *not* similar at all.

Still, as the saying went, she would just have to lie back and think, not of England, but of all the poor kids with cancer. How wonderful it would be to make their lives a little easier, to help their pain and to provide some hope. With those positive thoughts in mind, she could do *anything*…except surrender her pride any more than was necessary.

'I prefer not to ask Rico and Renée about you at all,' she replied curtly. 'I do not want them to know about this. Or anyone else, for that matter. I want to keep it a secret.'

'Really? I would imagine your very sexy public image would be enhanced if people found out that our dinner date had led to our having an affair.'

'Oh, *please*. Remember what I said about calling a spade a spade? This will not be an affair. It will—'

'How do you know?' he broke in, a challenging gleam in his black eyes. 'How do you know that we will not prove to be perfectly attuned to each other? You might enjoy yourself so much in my bed that you will not want next week ever to end.'

'You *are* mad,' she muttered just as the waiter came in with their entrées.

After the waiter had left, Charmaine stared down at her plate of prawns with no interest whatsoever. Her appetite was totally gone. Not so the prince's. He picked up his fork, speared a prawn and popped it

into his mouth, chewing slowly with an expression of sensual delight on his face.

'Eat up,' he said after he'd devoured two more in the same slow, almost erotic fashion.

'I'm not hungry,' she snapped.

His glance across the table showed impatience. 'I do not like women who sulk.'

'And I do not like men who force me into sleeping with them.'

'I am not forcing you, Charmaine. I never force women to sleep with me. You can still say no.'

'You know I can't. You *know* that.'

'Yes,' he agreed, his eyes glittering. 'Which only makes me want you all the more.'

She shook her head at him in utter bewilderment.

'There are many women in the world just as beautiful as I am, Your Highness, who could be had for a lot less money.'

'I am well aware of that. But it is *you* I want.'

'Why? Why *me*?'

He shrugged, but his eyes were far from casual. They locked on to hers across the candlelit table, deep, dark pools of the most amazing intensity. 'To be honest, I do not know why you. It is as much a mystery to me as it is to you. I am not normally attracted to women who flaunt themselves for all the world to see. But once I saw you, I simply had to have you. End of story.'

'Only because you had the money to buy me,' she derided. 'I would not be sitting here tonight if you'd been poor!'

His mouth pulled back into a drily amused smile. 'I beg to differ. If I had been poor, you would have looked upon me more kindly from the start. As it is,

for some reason my money and my position has blinded you to the mutual attraction which sizzles between us.'

'*What?* My, but you do have a high opinion of yourself, don't you? There is no mutual attraction sizzling between us, Your Highness,' she threw at him in caustic tones. 'I told you once before and I'll tell you again, I do not like you, and I am *not* attracted to you.'

'I agree you do not seem to like me, but you lie when you say you are not attracted to me. The woman I met at the races last year could not keep her eyes off me all day. And the woman who challenged me on that stage last Saturday night was charged with so much sexual electricity, I was almost burned by it. You do want me, Charmaine, even if you will not admit it to yourself. But time will overcome that small problem,' he finished up, then returned to eating his entrée, leaving Charmaine to stare at him in sheer amazement.

The man was deluded! Couldn't keep her eyes off him last year? It had been the other way around! And what she was charged with last Saturday night hadn't been sexual electricity but fury! Same as now.

Charmaine sat there in a stunned and speechless state whilst he devoured the last of his prawns, then dabbed elegantly at his mouth with his serviette before setting his arrogant gaze upon her once more.

'I am an excellent lover,' came his next astonishing remark. 'A woman of your experience will appreciate my expertise.'

Charmaine saw that arguing with this man was futile. 'I see modesty is not one of your virtues,' she sniped.

'I am just calling a spade a spade. I know my talents, as well as my shortcomings. I am gifted with horses, cards and women. But with women most of all.'

'Is that so? Interesting. Tell me, then, have you ever had a woman, Your Highness, who did not respond to your expert lovemaking?'

'No.'

Charmaine rolled her eyes. The man was not only deluded, but was also an egomaniac. 'Has it not occurred to you that some of your lady friends might have faked it because of what you could afford to buy them?'

He smiled a roguish smile. 'But of course. And I have no doubt some of them have, in the beginning. But in the end, they were all very genuine in their pleasure and satisfaction in my bed, even those who were shy and inhibited at the start. Women are no different from horses. Some come to the saddle as if they were born to it. Others resist. But skill and patience invariably wins the day.'

'So you are claiming a one hundred per cent success rate, both with women and horses?'

'There *was* a mare once. A rogue who had been mistreated as a filly. She was the closest I ever came to failure. She would rather have died than let me ride her.'

'I see,' she said drily. Sounded familiar. 'So what happened?'

'I was advised to put her down. But I can never do that, not unless the horse in question is injured beyond repair. Besides, even if she never raced, I intended keeping her for breeding.'

'So what *did* you do?'

'I put her in a yard by herself and became her personal groom. I fed her and mucked out her stall every day. And all the while, I talked to her. In the beginning, she wouldn't let me near her. She'd back away into a corner and snort and rear up. But I could see she was only bluffing. She didn't really want to hurt me. Horses are gregarious creatures and like company. I made sure I was her only company. After a while, she started hanging over the fence, watching and waiting for me. She let me touch her a little. First her head. Then her neck. And finally, her flanks. She would actually quiver with pleasure at my rhythmic stroking.'

A quiver ran through Charmaine at the thought of his stroking *her* flanks. But not a quiver of pleasure, surely. More likely revulsion.

'Soon, I literally had her eating out of my hand,' he went on. 'After that, the breaking-in process went quickly and easily. In the end, she loved being ridden, especially by me.'

Charmaine knew that would never happen with her. Even if he had five *hundred* days, rather than five, she knew the only emotions she would experience being ridden by him would be boredom and resentment. In a perverse fashion, it was going to be interesting to see what he'd do when she didn't respond to his so-called expertise. If she could get beyond the pride factor, then going to bed with the sheikh could prove an even better act of revenge than his. How would *he* feel, this lover extraordinaire, when he failed to arouse her, never mind satisfy her?

'So how much did she cost?' she asked. 'This mare you almost failed with.'

'A couple of million.'

'That's a lot of money. I can imagine you would go to great lengths not to see it wasted. But it's not nearly as much as the half a billion dollars you paid to have sex with me.' It amused her to think he'd really wasted his money this time.

He glared at her across the table, his expression affronted. 'I do not wish to have sex with you, Charmaine. I want to make love with you.'

'Whatever.' If he wanted to play the role of romantic lover then who was she to object? In truth, she was more than happy to indulge this particular fantasy of his. At least then he wouldn't want her to do gross things in bed. Not that she would, anyway. Even five hundred million dollars wasn't enough money for her cooperation in anything other than straight sex. She would have to make that quite clear at some stage before this evening was out.

'You must agree your offer was over-the-top,' she went on. 'You probably could have had me for less.'

'I did not want you to think I thought you cheap. I wanted to offer an amount which I thought was fitting.'

'Now, don't play *me* for a fool, Your Highness,' she countered, not at all conned by his flattering words. She wondered how many women had melted with his *I don't want to have sex with you, I want to make love with you* crap?

'You have no concern over what I think, or how I feel about this,' she went on. 'The reason you offered so much was because you knew it was an amount I couldn't turn down. That's the bottom line, isn't it? You didn't want me saying no to you again.'

He smiled a coolly enigmatic smile. 'You are ab-

solutely correct, Charmaine. That *was* the bottom line. I could not risk that happening. Not a second time.'

'Which brings us back to the main issue I have with you, Your Highness. You *are* a spoiled and arrogant man who has not had no said to him often enough.'

His gaze hardened on her again. 'Think what you will. Just be at my hotel suite on time tomorrow afternoon.'

Now was the time to put her foot down. To make her stance.

'Before I give my final word on this arrangement,' she said curtly, 'I want it understood that I will not be a party to any activity which I consider lewd, or kinky.'

He considered her thoughtfully for a few seconds, during which she had never felt more uncomfortable.

'Since I do not know what you would consider lewd or kinky, I will agree that you are perfectly free to say no to anything which makes you uncomfortable, or which you know you would not enjoy.'

She laughed. She couldn't help it. 'In that case, Your Highness, you are in for one very long, very boring and very frustrating week.'

His eyes showed both surprise and shock. 'Are you saying that you do not enjoy lovemaking?'

For a split-second, Charmaine worried that she had just ruined her chances of securing all that lovely money for her foundation. But then she remembered the sheikh's bottom line, and knew that he would not be able to resist having her, even if she said she was as frigid as an Antarctic ice-floe.

'Unfortunately, that is a fact, Your Highness. I do not enjoy sex. Not for want of trying, might I add. I have had several lovers over the years. All to no avail.

Of course, a man of your exceptional expertise,' she continued, a little wickedly, 'might have more success. I will await the moment of truth with bated breath.' The same way she awaited the moment the dentist gave her a needle.

He stared at her, his eyes assessing. 'You are mocking me,' he said.

'Think what you will, Your Highness.'

Again, his eyes searched her face. 'Is it the actual act of love that you do not enjoy, or everything that leads up to it as well? Would you object to my kissing your breasts, or other parts of your body?'

Charmaine sucked in sharply as images of those activities suddenly flooded her mind. She stared at his mouth and waited for the revulsion to kick in. Instead, an insidious heat swept over her skin at the thought of his hard, almost cruel-looking mouth roving all over her naked body, sucking on her nipples, kissing and exploring every intimate inch of her. Her stomach muscles clamped down hard and a tension such as she had never experienced before gripped all her insides. Her face flamed and her heartbeat fluttered wildly.

'I will take it by your reaction and your silence that you have no objections to foreplay,' he said. 'So I will make you this promise. I will not have actual intercourse with you till I am positive you will enjoy it. Fair enough?'

More than fair, she thought dazedly, and nodded her agreement. Impossible to talk, her tongue having cleaved to the roof of her mouth, her lips and throat as dry as the desert.

'Good,' he said. 'Now eat up.'

Ali watched her actually do as she was told for

once, well aware that something had just thrown her
out of kilter. Had she finally recognised what he had
known from the first moment of meeting her at the
races, that he was not the only one who was smitten?
Or had she been unexpectedly excited by the thought
of his doing the things he had described to her?

Her blush suggested some form of arousal. When
combined with the shock in her eyes he could only
conclude that her sexual response to him had really
surprised her.

But why would a woman this bold and this beautiful not normally enjoy making love?

Something must have happened to her in the past,
something that was blocking her pleasure in sex.
Some unpleasant or even traumatic personal experience.

As he'd said, women and horses had much in common. They were sensitive creatures, easily spooked,
easily spoiled, especially when young. What had happened when Charmaine was young to make her like
this?

Ali resolved to find out. First thing tomorrow
morning, he would contact the Sydney detective
agency he always used and ask them to run a more
thorough background investigation into the woman
sitting opposite him. They had already run a cursory
security check on her this week, which had shown
nothing of note to worry about regarding his own personal safety.

Now Ali would tell them to dig deeper, to go back
further and find out everything that had happened to
her since her birth, but to concentrate on her teenage
years. There had to be something to cause a woman

of her sensual nature and appearance to become frigid. He refused to believe she was born that way.

Not that she was really frigid. As he had already told her, he had *felt* her sexual response to him all along. It had been in her eyes, and her body language, sometimes subtly, sometimes flagrantly.

Her overt hostility towards him was not rational, and totally unwarranted by anything he had personally done to her. He had to find out what was causing it. He would get AIS to email a report update to him every day, and he would demand to know everything there was to know before the week was out.

Meanwhile, he would have to be patient, just as he had been with the rogue mare. As much as it would be difficult to keep his hands off Charmaine's beautiful body, he would do so to begin with…but only for a day or so. He knew he would not last any longer than that.

Ali sighed at the cold, hard reality of just how much having this woman would cost him. Was she worth it?

When she looked up from her entrée and set those incredible eyes of hers on him once more, his flesh leapt wildly and he knew it was worth every cent for him to find peace, both for his body and his mind. He had had enough of this obsession, or infatuation, or whatever it was he was suffering from. It had been going on for far too long.

Nothing during the past year—no other woman or other activity—had been able to drive this creature far from his thoughts. His desire for her was beyond desire. If fate had not put that auction in his path Ali did not know what he would have done. Kidnapped her, perhaps.

But fate had played right into his hands and now she was his. For five days; five days to seduce her to his will, to make sure that when their arrangement ran out she would still want him, even without his money.

Five days should be more than enough time. He usually had women melting for him after one night.

'You are not to worry,' he told her when she continued to look at him with fear in her eyes. 'I would never hurt you.'

Her eyes flashed and she drew herself up straight in her chair, sending him a look he had to admire. What courage she had. What spirit. What fire.

Impossible for her to be truly frigid!

'It would be *your* loss if you do, Your Highness,' she said with a proud toss of that gorgeous head of hair. 'Because if you hurt me, I will kill you.'

'You will not have to,' he returned ruefully. 'If I am stupid enough to hurt you, I will kill myself.'

CHAPTER FIVE

His helicopter was big and black. Ex-army, the prince told her as he guided her across the rooftop heliport towards the rather ominous-looking craft, made even more ominous perhaps by the thick black clouds gathering overhead.

The weather forecast had predicted a warm, muggy day for Sydney, followed by a late-afternoon storm. The thought of flying through rain and lightning did little for the savage knots that were already twisting in Charmaine's stomach.

'Do not worry about the weather,' he said when he saw her frown up at the sky. 'I checked the weather on the computer in my suite before you arrived. The radar map shows it is clear to the north of Sydney. The storm clouds are heading straight out to sea. If there was any danger, I would not allow the pilot to take off.'

Charmaine wasn't so sure about that. She had a feeling his royal highness would risk anything to whisk her off to the privacy of his property tonight. He'd made no attempt to hide the hunger in his eyes when she'd presented herself at the presidential suite less than fifteen minutes ago.

Yet she'd dressed down for the occasion even more than last night, choosing three-quarter-length fawn cargo trousers with a simple short-sleeved yellow shirt, not tucked in or tied at her waist to show off her toned midriff as she would normally have worn

it. Flat fawn sandals covered her feet. Minimal make-up graced her face. No jewellery adorned her ears, hands, wrist or neck, and the only perfume wafting from her body was the apple scent of her shower gel and shampoo.

But nothing, it seemed, would deter this man's lust for her. It was there, in his blazing black eyes as he'd hurried her up here with telling speed, sending her luggage ahead with a lackey. Obviously, he was anxious to get things underway.

She was, too, in a perverse kind of way. The last twenty-four hours had been hell. She hadn't slept or eaten since leaving the restaurant around ten-thirty. Though, after last night's dinner, perhaps that was just as well. How *had* she got through that meal?

After she'd made her melodramatic threat about killing him if he hurt her, and he'd come back with his rather ironic-sounding reply, the rest of the evening had become somewhat surreal. All discussion of the week ahead had ceased and the prince had chatted away to her quite nonchalantly through the next two courses, and then coffee afterwards. All quite innocuous topics, mostly to do with Australia. The economy. The weather. The up-coming elections. He'd also thankfully stopped staring at her as though he was dying of thirst in the desert and she was an oasis, which had enabled her to relax enough to make some intelligible contributions to the conversation.

But once she'd left his company and returned to her hotel room, the reality of what she'd agreed to came back with a rush and all hell broke loose in her mind. What *had* she been thinking of? *No* amount of money was worth doing what she had to do.

Her stomach had churned. Her skin had crawled.

Her head had whirled. She'd paced the hotel room for ages before finally plunging herself into a long, hot shower, searching for some way to relax her tightly strung-up body.

But what she'd discovered about herself in that shower had blown her mind much more than the arrangement she'd just entered into. The memory of her rock-hard nipples, plus the telling wetness between her legs, still had the power to shock her.

Charmaine's step faltered as she became aware that her nipples were *still* like iron pokers inside her bra.

Her face flamed at the realisation that the sheikh was right. She *did* want him. At least, her body seemed to. She still disliked him intensely. How could she not? But she was attracted to him, like a moth to the flame.

There was no sensible or intelligent reason behind the attraction. It was basic and primal. Something to do with the survival of the human species, she imagined. Eons ago, cavewomen had automatically chosen to mate with the caveman who would produce the best and strongest offspring, as well as having the power to protect them.

Charmaine could understand such a choice in the primitive and untamed past. But it had no place in the civilised world of today. The qualities *she* admired and respected in a man were not size, or strength, or even wealth and power, but kindness and tenderness, honesty and decency. What a pity her body didn't agree with her, she thought agitatedly as this dark and powerful man guided her towards the ladder that led up into his huge black helicopter.

No wonder she hadn't been able to sleep last night. But alongside her annoyance over this mortifying

situation lay the tiniest smidgeon of relief at discovering that maybe—just maybe—she was sexually normal after all. She'd just been going to bed with the wrong types. Whilst her brain had been drawn to nice guys, her traitorous body craved just the opposite.

But then, hadn't it always? she thought bitterly.

The sheikh's possessive grip on her elbow suddenly annoyed her and she threw him a savage glance over her shoulder. 'I can manage alone,' she snapped.

His deferential nod was not matched by the blaze of fire she encountered in his eyes. Clearly, she was trying his patience. Also clearly, he was eager to get her alone in his no doubt palatial residence up in the Hunter Valley so he could start seducing her.

Charmaine tried not to think about that moment, because it was fraught with so many mixed emotions. More so now because everything had changed. Last night, when she'd agreed to this liaison, she'd imagined herself lying like a log beneath him, enduring his sexual attentions with her usual lack of response, at the same time feeling triumphant that he would not have a chance in Hades of either seducing *or* satisfying her.

The new concept of his smugly discovering she *was* turned on by him appalled her, as did the prospect that she would not protest when he confidently moved from foreplay to the real thing. She hated the thought that she might actually enjoy everything he did to her.

If she told the therapist she'd consulted at one stage that she was repelled by the prospect of finally finding pleasure in sex, he would have called her truly mad. But it wasn't finding pleasure in sex itself that upset

Charmaine but finding pleasure in sex with this particular man, this…predator.

It was a most frustrating situation, but one she would have to address, come tonight. Or maybe even earlier, she realised with a jab of panic as she reached the top of the ladder and stepped into the ultra-luxurious interior of the royal helicopter.

'Good lord!' she couldn't help exclaiming as her eyes darted around. No upright seats jammed together in here. The place looked like an elegant sitting-room with large armchairs and a sofa that could easily have doubled for a bed. The colour scheme befitted royalty with lots of creams and golds. The walls and ceiling were lined with a rich wooden panelling, and the cream carpet was thick and plush.

'I had it especially fitted out to my requirements,' the prince said from just behind her shoulder. 'I fly a lot so I like to be comfortable. There is a fully equipped kitchen and bathroom on board as well. And a built-in bar for my guests. You will also notice once we are underway that this area is soundproofed. The noise of a helicopter this size is bone-rattling.'

'I suppose you have drop-dead-gorgeous flight attendants as well,' she said drily, waiting for one or two to make their appearance from behind the two closed doors at the back of the aircraft.

'Not on flights this short,' he returned smoothly. 'Nor when I have a special lady-friend with me.'

She turned to stare at him, even as the large outside door was banged shut behind them.

'You mean we…we are alone back here?' Alone, and no one able to hear her scream.

'Yes,' he said simply, his eyes searching hers. 'You have some objection to that?'

'Yes. No. No, I suppose not.' But she shuddered.

'Remember what I promised. I will not do anything you do not want me to do.'

'Well, I don't want you to touch me,' she said with an hysterical edge to her voice. *'Ever!'*

'You do realise that contravenes the terms of our arrangements,' he said coolly.

'Yes.'

'I could demand you comply.'

'You could try.'

He smiled. He actually smiled. 'I could. But that is not my way. I prefer to make love, not war. Still, if you want your foundation to have five hundred million dollars placed in its account tomorrow morning, then I would suggest you reconsider your attitude between now and the time of our arrival at my home.'

Charmaine winced at this reminder of why she'd agreed to do this. Here she'd been, getting carried away with her own selfish emotions and her own foolish pride again. What did it matter if this man thought he was God's gift to women? And what did it matter if she became just another of his one hundred per cent success rate with women?

The sheikh's satisfaction and her own mortification would be even greater, she reasoned, if she made a show of resisting, only to melt when he finally took her into his arms. Better she go to him willingly. Take the initiative—and some of the triumph—away from him.

All very common-sense logic, but she just could not do it. When he walked towards her she automatically shrank back a couple of steps, her reaction bringing him to a dead halt, his eyes betraying a surprising concern.

'I am not going to touch you,' he said brusquely. 'Not in the way you think,' he added, then pried her shoulder bag away from her desperately clutching hands and placed it on a nearby table. 'Sit down in one of those chairs and rest, Charmaine. You look tired.'

'That's because I haven't slept,' she snapped, and once again his eyes searched hers.

'In that case, lie down on the sofa and have a nap.'

'How can I possibly sleep when I have tonight hanging over my head?' she threw at him. 'Not to mention this whole week. Not only do I not enjoy sex, but I have never gone to bed with a man I didn't like.'

'In that case, I had better make sure you grow to like me very quickly,' he said drily, and moved off to the side where there was a built-in wall-unit of cupboards, opening one of the large upper doors and extracting two bed-sized pillows and a blanket. She blinked in surprise when he carried them over to the sofa and arranged them into a day bed for her.

He really was an incredibly graceful mover, she conceded reluctantly as her eyes followed his every move. With a great body.

Dressed as he was that afternoon in black jeans and a wine-coloured polo top, there was no hiding his fitness, or his shape. Charmaine had never liked overly big, bulky or muscle-bound men. She preferred men who were elegantly T-shaped, with wide shoulders, slender hips, long legs and washboard stomachs. Prince Ali had all that. And more, she realised.

She flushed and looked away, but the sight of him stayed in her mind, rattling her considerably. She recalled what the sheikh had said about his knowing

she wanted him because she had stared at him all day last year at the races. Which perhaps she had. And now he'd caught her staring at him again. No, lusting after him would be a better description.

Actions did speak louder than words and her actions kept contradicting her claims that she had no sexual interest in him.

'Come,' he ordered her. 'Your bed is ready.'

Her legs began to move in his direction before she could stop them, drawn by the power of his eyes and the sudden and urgent longing that swept through her like a tidal wave. She came closer and closer till she was within an arm's length of where he was standing by the sofa. What would happen, she wondered dazedly, if she just reached out to him, if she forgot everything else and just surrendered to the moment?

She almost did it. Almost lifted her hands to touch his face, and his hair. But then her pride kicked in again and her hands curled into fierce fists at her sides instead. When he saw them he scowled, whirled and stalked away from her. She watched him select the furthest armchair and ram his body into it, gripping the arm-rests angrily as he leant back. Only then did he glance back at her, his face grim.

'Lie down,' he commanded coldly.

Feeling oddly shattered and grateful at the same time, she almost fell down onto the sofa.

'Th...thank you,' she stammered as she lay back and pulled the blanket up to her suddenly shivery shoulders.

'Do not thank me yet,' he threw at her. 'Come tonight, you will not be let off so easily. You *will* let me touch you, madam. And you will do so willingly. Only then will we be able to get past all this nonsense.

Now go to sleep. That way you will be refreshed when we arrive.'

Ali was glad when she closed her eyes and did as she was told. Or appeared to. He tried to relax himself, but how could he when he was practically gnashing his teeth with frustration and irritation?

The woman was impossible, giving him mixed messages all the time. She wanted him. He *knew* she did. But nowhere near as much as he wanted her. Her claim that she never wanted him to touch her—*ever*—was patent rubbish. When she came up to him just now, she had been going to touch him. He had seen it in her eyes. But then something had happened and she had changed her mind.

A Western woman's pride, no doubt. Did she not know that women were made to touch and be touched? Women like her more than others. So soft. So exquisite. So passionate.

Oh, yes, she would be passionate in bed. She could pretend to be cold all she liked but Ali had seen the fire in her eyes when she looked at him. Besides, how could a body like hers not be responsive? Allah had made her for the delights of the flesh. Once he started kissing her, all that surface ice would melt away.

Tonight, he decided, abruptly abandoning his earlier resolve to wait a day or so before making love to her. To keep delaying the inevitable would only make her more difficult. Besides, the pain in his loins at the moment was excruciating. Frankly, he had never suffered the like, not even all those years ago when…

Ali's back and shoulders stiffened at this surprising thought. His hands curled over the arm-rests even tighter and his frown deepened. Had he really not felt like this all those years ago with Nadia? Surely his

need would have been worse, given he'd been younger then and so much in love.

But, to be honest, Ali could not recall his physical frustration back then ever being this intense.

Another startling realisation came to him as he was sitting there, thinking. He had not given Nadia a single thought since first setting eyes on Charmaine on television over a year ago. Not till this moment.

Did that mean he no longer loved his brother's wife? Or had time simply dimmed his memory of her to a point where he had forgotten how Nadia had once made him feel? No doubt if he saw her again, it would all come rushing back. The passion. The all-consuming love. The willingness to sacrifice everything, just to be with her.

But he would never see her again. That was the truth of it. His family—and hers—would never allow that. Nadia was now the wife of Crown Prince Khaled and mother to Khaled's son and heir, little Faisal. One day Nadia would be Queen of Dubar. Ali had no place in her life. His life was here now, in Australia, with his horses and his...

He glanced over at the figure huddled up on the sofa, her eyes shut, the blanket pulled up around her shoulders.

He had been going to say 'hobbies' in his mind. But Charmaine could hardly be classified as a hobby. She was an obsession, a tortured and tormenting obsession. She haunted his dreams and distracted his days.

As his gaze lingered on her lovely face, Ali's flesh leapt once more and he vowed darkly to make her his. He would use every sexual skill he had acquired over the years to seduce this contrary creature into

surrendering herself totally to him; to be enslaved by him; maybe even to fall in love with him.

A light flashed on in Ali's brain, brilliant and blinding in its shining truth. That was what he wanted most of all, wasn't it? For her to fall in love with him, to become as obsessed with him as he was with her.

But why? For what purpose? Revenge? Maybe it was his dark side, craving the opportunity to do to her what she had done to him. If she fell in love with him, he could have her in his bed for as long as he liked. And then, when he'd had his fill of her, he could discard and reject her as cruelly and carelessly as she had rejected him last year. *She* would be the one unable to sleep at night for wanting *him*. *She* would become the fool, driven to act without honour or pride. He could see her now, begging to see him again, crawling to him on her hands and knees and promising to do anything he wanted, if only he would let her back into his life.

Yes, he rather liked that scenario.

A glance at his gold Rolex showed they were still an hour away from their destination. Another glance at Charmaine showed the slight but steady rhythm of real sleep. She was resting. Good. She would need to be rested. She had a long night ahead of her.

CHAPTER SIX

A HAND gently shaking her shoulder had Charmaine bolting upright on the sofa, the blanket falling off her shoulders, and then onto the floor. The prince, who was leaning over her, bent to pick it up.

'We will be landing shortly,' he told her as he straightened and stepped back, the blanket in his hands. 'I thought you might like to freshen up before we do so.'

'What? Oh. Oh, yes. Yes, I would.' She pushed her hair back from her face then slowly swung her feet over the side of the sofa and stood up, amazed that she had actually fallen asleep. Maybe it had been the throbbing of the engines through the floor that had rocked her off to sleep. Or maybe just sheer exhaustion. Whatever, she did feel better than before. A little calmer. Less panicky.

'The bathroom is the door on the right.'

'Thank you,' she said and walked over to get her bag from the side-table the prince had put it on when they'd first boarded.

The feel of his black eyes burning into her back as she headed for the bathroom soon brought Charmaine right back to her earlier agitation. Not even closing the door behind her and blocking his gaze helped this time.

'Damn the man,' she told her reflection in the gold-framed vanity mirror.

By the time Charmaine emerged from the luxu-

riously appointed bathroom ten minutes later, the helicopter had landed and she was feeling a little more
in control.

I can do this, she told herself staunchly as she
headed for the exit door, which was now open. The
shame is all his, not mine, and she flashed the sheikh
a scathing look as she brushed past him.

He at least had the brains not to try to help her
down the ladder, for which Charmaine was grateful.
She suspected that she might react poorly to his finding excuses to touch her at this stage. Let him have
the decency to wait, she thought viciously, till they
were alone in his bedroom.

Charmaine was so consumed with her awareness of
him coming down the ladder behind her that she
didn't pay attention to her surroundings for a few seconds. But when she did, what she saw took her breath
away. Yet she couldn't see all that much. It was almost dark, with a bank of clouds blocking any moon
and stars. Most of the property remained hidden from
her view. Not so the magnificent white-stuccoed residence sprawled across a hilltop, a hundred or so me-
tres above where the helicopter had landed on a flat
section of land.

Despite having expected his residence to be palatial, Charmaine gazed up in awe at the mansion's size.

'Come,' the prince said from just behind her shoulder. 'We will ride up to the house.'

'Ride?' she echoed, swinging around in astonish-
ment. Till she saw the golf-style buggy awaiting
them.

A new lackey was already putting their cases in the
back. He looked Australian, not Arab, and, although
probably over thirty, had a strangely childlike ex-

pression on his weatherbeaten face. Once the cases were stowed away, he jumped in behind the wheel of the buggy, being careful, Charmaine noted, not to stare too hard or too long at her.

'Thanks, Jack,' the prince said as he climbed into one of the two empty back seats. 'Coming?' he directed at Charmaine, who was still standing there.

She climbed in beside him, and the buggy immediately lurched off, Charmaine clutching the hand rail in front of her to keep her balance. The last thing she wanted was to be thrown against the man next to her, who was already too close for comfort.

The sheikh chatted away to Jack during the drive up the rather steep gravel path, mostly about the storm in Sydney and what a lucky run they'd had so far with the weather that year. Nice spring rains, et cetera.

Jack, however, didn't say much in return. Just the occasional uh-huh. Although slightly miffed that she wasn't introduced, Charmaine was grateful for the opportunity to take in more of the property. Her eyes had grown accustomed to the dusk light by then and she could make out groups of buildings in the valley below. A river too, flanked by tall trees.

On each side of the river lay huge fields covered by a crop of some kind. Oats, maybe. Or lucerne. Further away from the river the land was less flat, the gently rolling hills marked out into paddocks of various sizes by white-painted wooden fences. Horse paddocks, obviously. Enclosing the valley were two tall mountain ranges, rising moodily and magnificently into the cloud-filled sky.

Despite the enthralling panorama of the landscape, Charmaine's gaze soon returned to the prince's house,

which they were rapidly approaching. It actually looked more like a convent than a house, with its cloistered verandas and myriad archways. Very Mediterranean. If she didn't know better, she would have thought she was in Spain, or Sicily.

At last they pulled up in front of several wide terracotta-tiled steps that led up onto a similarly tiled veranda and a simply huge front door, with an equally huge brass knocker. Dark wood the door was, the perfect foil for the starkly white walls of the house.

Charmaine scrambled out before the prince could stride around and gallantly take her hand, her motivation not escaping his attention, if the dry look he gave her was any indication. They walked together but apart up the steps whilst Jack bustled around with the luggage behind them.

A middle-aged woman with short spiky red hair opened the front door before anyone needed to use the brass knocker, her vivacious blue eyes sparkling with genuine welcome at Ali before widening slightly on Charmaine.

This time the prince actually deigned to introduce her.

'Cleo, this is Charmaine, whom I'm sure you'll recognise. Charmaine, this is Cleo, my housekeeper. Cleo has been with me for some years now.'

'How do you do?' Charmaine said politely.

'Delighted, I'm sure, love,' the housekeeper said breezily as she took Charmaine's hand in both of hers. 'Come in, come in.' And she drew Charmaine into the enormous, square-shaped foyer. 'Won't be a sec, love.' Patting her hand, she let it go and turned to Jack, who'd made it inside with the cases. 'Jack, you know where the cases go. The large black one in the

boss's rooms. The others belong to the lady. They go in the bedroom a bit further along. I've opened the door for you so you know which one. You can go out through the side-door when you're done, OK?'

Jack nodded and took off through an archway on Charmaine's left. Cleo turned back to give Charmaine a more thorough appraisal from top to toe.

'My, you're even more beautiful than you are on all those magazine covers!' she gushed. 'You will have to keep her under lock and key, Ali, or none of the men will get any work done whilst she's here.'

Charmaine was taken aback by the woman calling her royal employer by his first name, but she supposed they did have a long relationship, and it *was* awkward calling him Your Highness all the time.

Ali laughed, startling Charmaine. He'd never laughed before in her presence. It quite transformed him from menacing predator to easy-going charmer.

'You could be right, Cleo. I dare say Norm will suddenly find all sorts of excuses to attend to the roses in the garden beds around the house.'

'I have no doubt about that. Norm's always had an eye for a pretty woman.'

'Too true, Cleo. You only have to look at who he married. Norm is my gardener and Cleo's husband of thirty years,' he explained to Charmaine, who was still amazed by his total change of manner. Suddenly, there was nothing royal or arrogant about him. He was even talking less pompously.

'Oh, go on with you,' Cleo scoffed. 'I'm fast becoming an old bag. Turned fifty the other week, love,' she told Charmaine. 'Took myself off to the hairdresser's in a bid to turn back the clock and came

home with this.' And she gesticulated to her hair. 'Come on, tell me the truth. What do you think?'

'I think it looks great. I wouldn't have taken you for a day over forty.'

Cleo beamed. 'I knew you were a girl of perfect class and taste the moment I clapped eyes on you. You can keep this one, Ali.'

'Thank you, Cleo. But I think Charmaine might have something to say about that.' And he threw her a wry smile.

Charmaine smiled back, more for Cleo's benefit than his. Charmaine liked the woman and didn't want to make her suffer for her boss's wickedness.

'I presume you have already followed through on my earlier instructions?' he asked the housekeeper.

Charmaine frowned. Earlier instructions? What earlier instructions?

'Everything is as you wanted, Ali. I will bring the food along shortly.'

'Good.'

When he turned and took her elbow, Charmaine stiffened, but the look on his face suggested she not make a fuss in front of Cleo, and she reluctantly complied, allowing him to guide her down the same dome-roofed, terracotta-tiled hallway that Jack had scuttled along earlier and which seemed to stretch into infinity.

'What earlier instructions?' she asked archly as he directed her past several shut doors on either side.

'Nothing for you to get stirred up about. I rang Cleo before leaving Sydney to tell her that I was bringing a special lady-friend home for the week and that we would be eating dinner tonight in my quarters.'

'You obviously didn't tell her my identity during this call.'

'Obviously not.'

'I dare say she's used to you bringing women home with you from your weekend sojourns to Sydney.'

'It is not an unknown situation. But you are by far the most famous and the most beautiful lady to have ever graced these halls.'

Charmaine snorted. 'I noticed she called you Ali. I'm surprised that you allow a servant to treat you with such familiarity.'

'Cleo is not a servant,' he corrected her coolly. 'She is an employee.'

'Pardon my mistake. I thought royalty always considered their employees servants.'

'I regret to say that is the case back in Dubar. But not here. Here, on this property, I am not treated like some pampered prince. Here, I have chosen to earn my respect. Admittedly, I am still the boss, but to a lot of the people who work for me I am also their friend.'

'Admirable sentiments. But I would not be too fooled if I were you, Your Highness. In my experience, the rich and famous rarely have true friends among the people who work for them.'

'That is a very cynical point of view.'

'Aah, but I am a very cynical lady.'

'Yes, I have noticed that. But cynicism, like any negative state of mind, can feed on itself and become self-destructive. I know this for a fact. When I first arrived on these shores I was a very cynical young man. But I soon discovered that if I wished to be successful and relatively content with my life here, I would have to try to adopt the Australian way of life,

which is far more laid-back and informal than anything I was previously used to. Admittedly, I find I fall back into old ways when I am out in public, or in the company of my wealthy city friends, but after I come home here I am soon a different man.'

'*Relatively* content?' she echoed, picking up on the innuendo behind the word. 'That sounds as though you'll never be really happy living here in Australia. Why stay, then, if that's the case? If you miss Dubar so much, why don't you just go back?'

'Now, you surprise me, Charmaine. Or possibly you disappoint me, since you have not even been curious enough to find out the most basic facts about my past. It is quite well known, in racing circles anyway, that I did not leave Dubar voluntarily. I was exiled.'

'Exiled!' Charmaine ground to a halt, throwing a startled glance up into his face. 'But…but why?'

His smile was enigmatic. 'There are many rumours, the most common being that I was discovered in a married woman's bed chamber whilst her husband was absent.'

'And the truth?' she asked.

'The truth is the girl in question was not yet married, just betrothed. Unfortunately, her husband-to-be was my oldest brother, Crown Prince Khaled.'

'Oh! And you actually slept with her?'

'I fully intended to. But I was discovered before the joyous event, and put on the next plane out of the country. My brother was lied to over the circumstances of my hasty departure. He was told I had become dangerously infatuated with a married woman on the royal staff and that I had been exiled for my own safety.'

'I see.' Charmaine nodded, well aware that adultery in his country was one of the gravest sins. People were executed for such transgressions.

'It wasn't just a one-sided infatuation though, was it?'

'No. Nadia loved me as much as I loved her. Or I thought she did. But she married Khaled within days of my exile and has had a son by him. From what I have heard, the marriage is a happy one.'

'Are you still in love with her?' she asked.

'Do you care?' he returned, his eyes searching hers.

Charmaine blinked. *Did* she?

'I was just curious,' she insisted. 'It would perhaps explain why a man such as yourself has never married. Living as you do here on this property, surely a wife would suit your purposes better than an endless stream of female…companions.'

'Aha, so you do know a little of my reputation.'

'I was warned about you.'

'Warned? What an interesting word! Warned. But a very apt one, on this occasion. You should have taken notice of whoever warned you. I presume it was Enrico. No, do not bother to deny it, my dear Charmaine. He would be the only one who would dare. But to answer your earlier question, yes, I loved her very much. More than my life was worth. I was willing to risk anything—even death—to be with her. I am a very passionate man, as you will have an opportunity to discover tonight…first-hand,' he finished oh, so softly.

Charmaine stared at him.

He stared right back, his black eyes burning. But were they burning for her, or was there another reason for his sexual obsession with her?

'Do I…remind you in some way of Nadia?' she asked, her mouth drying as she waited for his answer.

His gaze travelled slowly down her body then up again, making her quiver inside.

'Not in the slightest.'

Charmaine heard the hard edge in his voice.

'Come,' he said abruptly, and grabbed her arm again. 'The past is the past, Charmaine. Believe me when I say it has no effect on me any more.'

In a pig's ear, she thought as he shepherded her rather roughly down the corridor. He was as affected by his past as she was by hers. Clearly, his paying an exorbitant amount of money for her was a direct result of his having once been, maybe not rejected as such, but unable to have the woman he most desperately wanted. On this occasion, Charmaine's surface beauty had inspired a savage lust in him and nothing was going to stop him satisfying that lust this time. It might not be love driving him, but it was a powerful force all the same. She could feel it, vibrating through his arm and down into hers, making her stomach tighten and her heart race.

Not before time he stopped in front of a wooden door on the right and let go of her arm. Any further and his fingers would have bruised her skin.

His facial expression was grimly determined as he reached out for the brass knob, turned it and pushed the door open, waving her inside with an impatient gesture. Her tension increased considerably as she went in, but the sight that met her eyes totally threw her.

She'd expected a bedroom, but not one quite like this.

'This will be your room during your stay,' he an-

nounced curtly, walking past her and across the expanse of pale pink carpet to where white-painted double French doors led out on to another cloistered veranda. When he opened them, a pleasant breeze wafted in, ruffling the gauzy white material that was draped around the white-painted four-poster bed.

Charmaine stared at the very pretty bed with its pink lace quilt and matching pillowcases. For the life of her she could not imagine herself and the sheikh in it together. This was a bed designed for romance and relative innocence, a room for softness and tenderness, *not* the kind of sex that was going to transpire between them during the next five days.

Charmaine already knew that their encounters weren't going to be at all romantic and innocent, let alone soft and tender.

'That door leads to your walk-in wardrobe and *en suite* bathroom,' he said, indicating a door to the left of the bedhead. 'I am sure you will find everything in there you could possibly need. And this one...' he walked over to a door in the centre of the wall opposite the bed and flung it open '...leads to my personal quarters.'

Charmaine almost laughed at her own stupidity. Of course, this wasn't the sheikh's bedroom. This was a lady's retreat, not a setting designed for sin and seduction. No doubt his room would contain an even bigger bed and other accessories to enhance the sort of erotic experiences a man of his sophistication would enjoy.

'I will expect you to join me there, suitably clothed, in half an hour,' he pronounced brusquely. And with a curt bow of his darkly handsome head he turned

and disappeared into the short connecting hallway, shutting the door behind him.

Charmaine glared after him, the smidgeon of sympathy he'd evoked with his sad tale of lost love and bitter exile evaporating with his peremptory commands.

'Suitably clothed indeed,' she bit out before whirling and marching over to the door he'd said led into the walk-in wardrobe and bathroom.

Her two bags were already sitting on deep shelves in the more than adequate wardrobe. She angrily reefed them open, extracted what she needed for the night ahead then marched on through the next door.

The bathroom proved to be as pretty as the bedroom. All white tiles, with pink accessories and silver fittings. Above the white-tiled vanity bench ran a huge silver-framed mirror that slid back to reveal shelves containing an impressive assortment of toiletries.

A spa bath graced one corner of the room. A roomy shower filled another, and a toilet and bidet occupied a third. Unlike some less well-equipped bathrooms, this one had several towel rails sporting a large selection of plush pink towels. There was also a laundry basket with a sign on it saying that any clothes deposited would be cleaned, ironed and returned the same day.

Talk about spoiling one's guests!

Well, he could afford such indulgences, Charmaine supposed as she took a shower cap out of its packet then fitted it over her hair. Anyone who could afford to pay five hundred million dollars for five days' sleeping with some woman he fancied had to be ob-

scenely rich. Still, as the saying went, you can buy sex but you can't buy love.

Not that the sheikh wanted love these days. Clearly, his heart was back in Dubar with his brother's wife. The heart that beat in his chest today was as hard as nails. You didn't have to be a genius to work that out.

What he wanted from the women he brought here had nothing to do with love.

'Suitably clothed, eh?' she repeated with a laugh as she stripped off and dropped every single item of her clothing into the laundry basket before stepping into the shower. There she lathered herself all over with the perfumed shower gel she found in the recess in the shower wall. Then she turned the water to cold and let the icy rain beat upon her body till she was shivering.

By the time she switched off the taps she figured she'd thoroughly deheated herself, although her stunningly erect nipples didn't seem to reflect that idea. Charmaine was annoyed with herself for not remembering what ice did to her nipples. She'd used that trick only recently during a lingerie photo-shoot to make herself look sexier.

As she towelled herself down, she also regretted ever telling the sheikh that she didn't like sex. How much easier this would have been if he'd thought she was a promiscuous tart right from the start. Now he looked upon her as a sexual challenge.

No way could she allow him the triumph of thinking he'd expertly seduced her with his boudoir skills. Since she was condemned to be turned on by him, whether she wanted to be or not, then she aimed to make the running here, not him!

Charmaine donned the outfit she'd brought into the

bathroom with her, then opened her make-up bag and
went to work.

Finally, she was ready. Standing up straight, she
inspected her reflection in the mirror.

Perfect, she decided, although a shudder did ripple
down her spine at the sight she made. The negligee
set she'd chosen to wear tonight was one she'd mod-
elled recently for Femme Fatale's summer collection.
The nightie was long and made of red satin, its low-
cut halterneck bodice clinging like a second skin, the
rest falling to the floor in slinky folds. It almost could
have doubled as an evening gown, although a very
provocative one, especially with the way her braless
breasts and stunningly erect nipples were shamelessly
displayed by the unlined satin.

The overlay was pure Hollywood. Transparent
chiffon, with its hem and three-quarter-length sleeves
edged in red-dyed ostrich feathers. On her feet were
matching red satin high-heeled slippers that showed
her toes, now painted the same scarlet as her mouth.

The whole outfit was over-the-top and in-your-face
sexy. With the amount of make-up she had on, she
looked like an expensive call-girl.

'Yes, perfect,' Charmaine repeated ruefully.

Squaring her slender shoulders, she whirled and left
the bathroom. It was time to face the music. Time to
pay the piper, but not to play the helpless victim. Oh,
no. That part had been played once in her life, and
would never be repeated.

CHAPTER SEVEN

CHARMAINE'S steely resolve lasted till the sheikh swept open the door to his quarters.

Did she gasp?

She hoped not. But her eyes definitely widened.

Till that moment, she hadn't given a thought to what *he* might be wearing this evening. Her focus had all been on her own appearance.

But the sheikh's bedroom attire definitely rivalled hers in the provocative department. His long black silk pyjama bottoms were slung dangerously low on his hips, the matching knee-length robe hanging so wide open she could see all of his bare, bronzed chest right down past his navel.

Clearly, he'd not long been out of the shower as his head was still shiny and wet. His feet were bare and the hair on his chest had gathered into masses of tiny damp curls.

She stared at them, her fingers itching once more to touch him, to touch all of him. Dear heaven, but he was beautiful. More beautiful than any man had a right to be. Such thick, glossy black hair. Such gorgeous olive skin. Not to mention his lean, hard, masculine body.

But most magnetic of all were still his eyes, those eyes which at this very moment were blazing with a heat and a hunger that challenged her determination to remain hard and cold in his presence.

Her own blood ignited, making the entire surface

of her skin come alive. Her brain bubbled with a feverish excitement and the most corrupting thoughts. The idea that soon she *could* be touching him, and being touched *by* him, almost tipped her into a state of meltdown.

Charmaine felt her cheeks begin to burn, which pricked her pride back into action. How could she do this? Melt for this man like some infatuated virgin. It would be the ultimate humiliation.

No. She could not do it. She would not do it. Not for all the money in the world!

With a defiant tilt of her chin, she brushed past him and took a few steps into the room, putting some physical distance between them before announcing her decision.

For a split-second she was distracted by the room itself, which was so unlike what she was expecting. Much more casual and cosy. Forest-green carpet and warm cream walls. A fireplace. Built-in bookcases and lots of comfy-looking furniture. In the big bay window sat a glass dining table, looking very inviting, with fresh flowers surrounding a candle in the middle, the perfect setting for a romantic dinner *à deux*. A stainless-steel traymobile was positioned next to the table, presumably containing their evening meal.

'Do you wish to sit down and eat dinner straight away?' he asked, and she whirled to face him once more.

'What I wish, Your Highness,' she said stiffly whilst her heart raced and her stomach churned, 'is to put a stop to this charade once and for all.'

His face darkened. 'Meaning?'

'Meaning I have changed my mind. I can't do this. I am going back to my room to get dressed and re-

packed. I expect you to have me flown back to Sydney tonight.'

His dark eyes glittered ominously. 'Just like that.'

'Yes. Just like that.'

He said nothing. But his body language spoke volumes.

He wasn't going to let her go. Rico had warned her. Why hadn't she listened to him?

'I'm sorry to have inconvenienced you,' she choked out, and bravely headed for the door. Unfortunately, she had to pass the prince on the way.

For a moment, she thought she was safe. But then his right hand shot out, grabbing her left wrist and yanking her back round to land hard against him.

As usual when cornered, Charmaine came out fighting. Her own right hand swung wildly and connected with his cheek. She would have hit him again if his other hand hadn't secured that wrist as well.

'Let me go,' she bit out in fury as he bent both her arms around behind her back. 'Or I'll scream the place down.'

'Scream away. This house has thick stone walls and plate-glass windows, which you will note are closed, since the air-conditioning is on. Even if some sound could escape, there is no one nearby to hear. Cleo and her husband have driven into town to go to the movies. So you are as alone with me in here as you were in my helicopter.'

His hands tightened around her wrists and dragged her arms down straight, giving her a sobering glimpse of his physical strength.

Charmaine realised that fighting him was futile. Despite all her workouts in the gym, she was no match for this man. All she had to bargain with was

her brain, because she refused to involve her body, that body which even at this moment longed to submit to his.

What a traitor her flesh was! How it loved the way it was moulded to his, thigh to thigh, hip to hip, breast to chest. With him in his bare feet and her in heels, even their faces were dead level. How easy it would be to fit her mouth to his, to open her lips and accept his tongue. Just as easy to invite a far more intimate invasion.

Charmaine shuddered in shame at the excitement she experienced at the thought of doing just that.

'You…you assured me once you would never take a woman against her will,' she blurted out.

'I haven't. And I never will.'

'Then let me go.'

'You agreed to foreplay,' he reminded her.

'Is this kind of manhandling your idea of foreplay?'

'If I let you go, you will try to run away. Yet I know that is not what you want. You want me to touch you and kiss you. You want me to make love to you.'

'You're dead wrong. I *don't* want you to make love to me.' *Because I don't want you to find out that my body does!*

'Then what is it you want? To make love to me?'

'What? No! No, of course not.' Just the thought made her feel faint. 'I told you,' she protested in one last desperate gesture of defiance, 'I don't like sex. And I don't like you!'

'You will,' he promised, and actually had the gall to smile a little as his mouth descended.

She tried to keep her lips shut beneath his. Tried to resist. But her struggles defeated her even more

than if she'd stayed perfectly still. Moving her head from side to side only increased the delicious friction created by their mouths being clamped together. As for wriggling her lower body...

Total disaster!

For her movements simply provided her with a perfect mental imprint of his erection, which was formidable in a way that sent her head spinning. Could he really be that long and that thick, and that hard?

He gripped her wrists tighter and pressed her hands firmly against her bottom—possibly in an attempt to still her struggles. She froze in shock, but by then the soft swell of her stomach was wrapped snugly around his swollen sex, and her mouth had gaped open a little.

His tongue immediately slid inside. Not roughly or brutally. Slowly and confidently.

He tasted of mint, and of triumph.

And why not? Despite her earlier resolve, she *was* melting. And her pride was nowhere to be seen. In its place was a powerful urge to simply sink against him and let nature take its course.

Her sigh of surrender could not be mistaken. Perhaps because it was more of a moan than a sigh, a sensual sound that echoed in her mouth and told him that she was his for the taking.

His mouth lifted and their eyes locked, hers glazed, his gleaming. But he still did not let her go.

'Kiss me,' he whispered. 'Kiss me where you hit me.'

Charmaine stared at his still reddened cheek, then deep into his eyes. If they'd been angry, or arrogant, the erotic spell he was weaving might have been broken. But they weren't. They were softly smouldering,

and almost slumberous, his eyelids heavy with arousal.

His cheek felt hot under her lips. Hot and slightly bristly. His beard was beginning to grow. She liked the feel of the stubble under her already sensitised lips, rubbing her mouth across the rough surface, not once but several times. When her tongue darted forth and licked his cheek, a violent shudder rippled down her spine.

Shock had her face jerking away from his, their eyes meeting once more.

'You liked that, didn't you?' he said.

'Yes,' she agreed, though with some confusion. What was it about this man that she would even enjoy licking his stubbly skin? Was it the man himself? His masterfulness, or just the situation she found herself in?

Maybe she was secretly turned on by his having paid half a billion dollars to have sex with her. Maybe she liked the fact that she didn't have to like him. Maybe the secret to her sexual success here was that she could distance herself from any emotion which made her vulnerable.

Whatever the reason, there was no turning back. It would take a team of wild horses to drag her out of here now. She had to know what it would be like with him. *Had* to.

'Do not worry,' he murmured, and bent to brush his lips with tantalising tenderness over hers. 'You will like doing many more things before this night is over.'

His abruptly releasing her arms disorientated her for a few seconds. She even experienced a jab of disappointment at her physical freedom. The thought that

she had enjoyed his holding her captive like that was a worry, as was his declaration that she would like doing many more things. Her mind boggled at the various images that came to mind. Yet alongside her shock lay a dizzying excitement and a desire to experience simply everything there was to be experienced with this man.

Such thinking really stunned her. This wasn't like her. Over the past few years she'd stopped being desperate to like sex and simply become uninterested. Bored, even.

His hands easing the red chiffon robe back off her shoulders catapulted Charmaine's mind out of her mental bewilderment and back on to the physical present. She quivered when his fingertips brushed over her collar-bones.

'You wore this outfit to provoke me,' he said as the flimsy robe fell down her arms and pooled at her feet.

She could not deny it.

'It worked,' he added before his fingers went to the straps on her nightie.

Charmaine tensed. Surely he didn't mean to strip her naked, here, in the middle of his sitting-room?

What *then*? Was she to eat dinner with him in the nude?

Was she repelled by that thought? Or turned on by it?

'It makes you look like a whore,' he ground out, and the nightie joined the negligee on the floor, leaving her standing before him in nothing but those red satin high heels.

He took a backward step, sucking in as his eyes seared over her nakedness. She stood there stiffly,

stung by his saying she looked like a whore. Even though it was true.

But perhaps that was what she had become? For as he stared at her, she grew more hotly aware of her female body than she had ever been before. Her skin seemed to glow under his white-hot gaze. Her breasts grew heavier. Her nipples tightened further.

When his gaze travelled further down her body, her belly contracted. Was he looking at her recently waxed pubis and despising her for going to such lengths for her career? Or did he think she'd done it for him?

'You are far too beautiful for your own good,' he muttered angrily. 'And far too brazen.'

With that, he swept her up into his arms and carried her towards his bedroom.

CHAPTER EIGHT

HIS bedroom was as unexpected in décor as his sitting-room. Not an erotically designed boudoir of the Arabian-nights variety at all, but a classy, relaxing retreat.

The walls were covered in a claret-coloured, suede-style wallpaper, its rich darkness relieved by subtle gold wall lights shining down on gilt-framed photographs of racehorses. The carpet was a deep gold and the bed was larger than any bed Charmaine had ever seen, its enormous rosewood bedhead flanked by matching bedside tables on which stood brass lamps with gold shades. The bed's cream and gold brocade bedspread had been thrown back, exposing cream satin sheets and matching pillows.

'What about dinner, Your Highness?' she dared to venture as he laid her down across those cream satin sheets.

His calling her brazen had revived some of her usual boldness. Or so she told herself. More likely her attempt at conversation was a desperate ploy to delay the discovery the sheikh was about to make, which was that she *did* want him.

'Dinner can wait,' he pronounced as he straightened and ripped off his own robe. 'And you are to stop calling me Your Highness. My name is Ali.'

'Whatever. You've paid for the privilege.'

He scowled at her impertinence, plus the reminder of how she'd come to be lying naked on his bed in

the first place. After a savage yank at the cord on his waistband, his black silk pyjama trousers dropped to the floor.

Charmaine gulped. Now she knew why he'd always been so successful with women. Prince Ali of Dubar certainly had an unfair advantage over the other men Charmaine had been to bed with. And most others, she suspected.

But the sheikh's flagrant masculinity—and possibly promiscuous lifestyle—rang warning bells in her head. She wasn't that far gone yet that she would take stupid risks just to find out if she could enjoy sex with this lover *extraordinaire*. Fortunately she was on the Pill, so pregnancy wasn't in the equation. But pregnancy was not the only consideration in this modern world.

'One thing before you start,' she said, proud that she could still find a steady voice in the face of such a sight. 'I do hope you have protection handy, because I *will* have to go home if you're not prepared to practise safe sex.'

'There are two full boxes in there,' he said with a curt nod towards the right-hand bedside table. 'And some loose under these pillows at the ready.'

Charmaine did her best not to look stunned. Now that she had refound some spirit, she refused to revert to mindless mush. But two full *boxes*? And more under the pillows? With *this* man? Hopefully, he didn't mean to use them all tonight or she wouldn't be able to walk tomorrow, let alone go horse-riding.

'The condoms I buy are custom designed,' he continued. 'They are also one hundred per cent pregnancy proof. I, too, have a passion for protection.'

'Yes, I imagine that a man of your obscene wealth

couldn't be too careful. But you don't have to worry about me trying to trap you. I already have a good chunk of your money and the last thing I would want is your baby.'

Too late she realised he might take her remark as a personal insult. Probably had, by the flash of fury in his eyes.

The thought upset her for some reason. Silly, really. He deserved an insult or two, this man who thought he could buy her body. And had.

But she still felt compelled to apologise.

'I…I'm sorry, Ali. I didn't mean that the way it sounded. I mean…it doesn't have anything to do with you. I just don't want *any* baby.'

Ali stared down at her distressed eyes and saw that she was, indeed, sorry. He sighed and shook his head. What a complex creature she was. Ali wished he understood what made her act in so many contradictory ways. Why had she come to him tonight dressed like a whore, only to then tell him she'd changed her mind about staying the week with him?

He'd been in danger of losing it when she'd said that. Almost had, till he realised she was just afraid of sleeping with him for some reason. Afraid of sex.

All that was needed then was a little gentle persuasion to change her mind back again. For a while, she'd become the woman he knew she could be in his arms. All liquid heat and trembling passion. Now she'd reverted to that other colder, bolder creature, the one who challenged him and made him want to act like some animal with her.

But that was not his way with women. He hated the thought of being reduced to a savage beast, some-

thing she seemed capable of doing. He only had to glance down at himself to see what she had reduced him to.

Delaying his own satisfaction was going to be difficult. But not impossible.

Now, how best to proceed to win her? Because that was his goal, wasn't it? To win her. To have her coming back for more at the end of these five days, *without* any monetary bribe.

Ali bitterly regretted not having had her background thoroughly investigated right from the start. Knowledge was power, and more than anything else he wanted to have power over her. But he was in the dark where Charmaine was concerned.

One thing Ali *did* understand about the naked woman lying before him was that the main thing keeping her in this room at this moment was the half a billion dollars it would earn her foundation. In other circumstances, he might have taken more time with her, as he had with that difficult mare.

But there was no time to waste. Five days wasn't all that long…

Charmaine's whole body tensed when he stepped forward and picked up her right foot from where it had been dangling over the side of the bed.

'Relax,' he murmured, his left hand encircling her ankle whilst his right hand slid up and down her calf with the lightest of feather touches. When he bent forward slightly to caress the sensitive skin behind her knee, goose-bumps broke out over her arms.

Relax! How could she relax whilst he was doing that to her and standing before her without a stitch of clothing on? Her eyes kept going to that part of him

she kept imagining inside her. *If* it would fit inside her.

Finally his hand returned to her foot, where he removed her red slipper and tossed it aside. He seemed to take longer on her left leg before removing that shoe, by which time she was trembling.

'Ali...'

She hadn't meant to speak. Hadn't meant to sound so desperate and needy.

His eyes went to hers. 'Yes?'

'Don't...don't make me wait too long.'

He nodded, then moved to scoop her up again in his arms and place her in the centre of the bed with her head on the pillows. She watched, wide-eyed, whilst he retrieved a condom from under a pillow and protected them both with a couple of well-practised moves. Her heart was thundering in her chest by the time he joined her on the bed and stretched out beside her.

'You don't want me to pleasure you with my mouth first?' he asked, his face looming over hers.

Charmaine blinked up at him. Did she?

'I...I don't know...'

He frowned at her uncertainty.

'Maybe a little,' she added breathlessly.

What was she *saying*?

But too late. He was already on his way, although not without an immediate detour to her breasts, where he suckled long and languorously on each nipple, leaving them stiff and wet and herself all twisting inside with the most excruciating need. By the time he moved on, she wanted him everywhere. On top of her. Inside her. Sucking her. Kissing her. Touching her.

'Oh,' she moaned when his tongue-tip swirled into her navel.

Who would have thought that could feel so delicious? She was so glad when he did it again. And again.

Her hands reached down to touch his hair, to run her fingers through it, luxuriating in its glossy softness. He glanced up briefly to smile at her before moving further down her body, licking over the smooth surface of her pubic bone whilst he pushed her thighs apart.

Her belly tightened in anticipation of his mouth reaching her exposed sex, and when it did she almost jackknifed off the bed.

'Sshhh,' he soothed, and reached up to press a large palm flat down on her lower stomach. 'Be still. Relax.'

More ridiculous commands. Impossible to be still, *or* to relax. His tongue was now circling her core, his fingers penetrating her. The sensations were both exhilarating and frightening, like being on a rollercoaster ride.

'Ali,' she choked out, and he immediately stopped.

She almost burst into tears, like a child whose lollipop had been snatched away.

But there was little time for ongoing dismay as he slid back up her body and started penetrating her for real. Her sharp intake of breath was a combination of pleasure and surprise. For despite his being bigger than any man she'd ever been with before—by far— she was able to accommodate him quite easily. Maybe even better if she...

When she lifted her legs and wrapped them high around him, he groaned. She did too, feeling the dif-

ference straight away. He was now very deep inside her, filling her entirely, evoking a stunning awareness of their fused flesh. Lord knew what it would feel like when he started to move.

She cried out when he started pumping back and forth, each forward movement ramming the head of his penis against her cervix.

He stopped again. 'I am in too deep,' he said.

'No, no, it's fantastic!'

'You are sure?'

'Absolutely. Don't stop.'

He laughed, then continued.

She climaxed in no time, with great, racking spasms of rapturous release, making her almost scream with pleasure. He clasped her tightly to him and came as well, his mouth opening with his own primal roar.

When she felt his flesh pulsating deep inside her, a sudden wave of decidedly primitive passion swept through Charmaine and she started kissing his shoulder, his neck and finally his gasping lips, sending her tongue deep into his mouth in an erotic echo of the way he'd penetrated her. He kissed her back and kept on moving, through his climax and her own, till astonishingly she came again. Only when she was completely done did he stop, his body collapsing on top of hers.

He was heavy but she didn't mind. She relished being enveloped by his body. She ran her hands possessively up and down his back and tried to remember why it was she didn't like him.

And then it came back to her.

He was a sexual predator who'd bullied her into

sleeping with him. Bullied and bribed and emotionally blackmailed her.

She could never tell him how grateful she was that he had. She had to find other words to explain her pleasure in his body, and to regain at least some of her pride.

'You see?' he murmured some time later as he lay beside her, one hand propping up his head whilst his other played idly with her breasts. 'You do like sex. At least you do with me.'

Charmaine, whose brain had been working overtime whilst her body had thrummed with pleasure at his tweaking her nipples, had fortunately come up with just the right reply.

'I have to confess my response to you surprised me at first. But I've since realised what turned me on so much. It's a popular female fantasy, you know, being paid a small fortune by some billionaire to have sex with them. Every woman has a secret yen to play the call-girl. And then there's the sheikh factor, of course.'

His hand stilled on her breast. 'The sheikh factor?'

'Don't act the innocent with me, Ali. I'll bet you've taken advantage of it many times. You know. The sheikh? Rudolph Valentino, sweeping the fair lady off to his desert lair to have his wicked way with her? That scenario has turned countless Western women on no end over the years. Don't pretend you don't know that.'

She finally dared to look up into his eyes, which remained annoyingly unreadable.

'And does it turn *you* on no end?' he said, plucking at her nipple once more, though not as gently as he had been doing.

Unfortunately, this seemed to excite her all the more.

'Who knows?' She shrugged, struggling to stay cool when all she wanted to do was beg him to make love to her again, to use her even more roughly this time. 'Something did. It certainly wasn't romance that got me going. Or love.'

'You don't find me romantic? Or lovable?' he added with another less than gentle tug on her other nipple.

She had to laugh. 'Oh, come, now, Ali. Paying a woman half a billion dollars to force her to be at your sexual beck and call for a week is hardly romantic, or lovable.'

'I didn't force you.'

Thank goodness he stopped with the nipple torture.

'As good as. You knew I wouldn't say no.'

'But you enjoyed yourself just now.'

'You would have demanded your pound of flesh whether I did or not.'

'No,' he said. 'I would not have.'

She stared up at him, not sure if he was telling the truth or not. Hard to believe that a man who had physically restrained her earlier tonight would have let her go if she hadn't been so easily seduced.

She shrugged. 'Whatever. It's of no consequence any more. It seems I like playing paid sex slave to your master. So, till Friday, I am yours to command. Command away, then, lover. The night, as they say, is still young.'

His eyes glittered in that way which had once made her angry but which now sent her breathing haywire. 'A sex slave does not demand her master command her,' he said in a soft, low, wickedly seductive voice.

'A sex slave remains silent and submissive and awaits his desire. A sex slave has no will of her own, surrendering it to her master's. She is nothing till he deigns to use her body. Nothing at all.'

Her mouth had grown dry as he spoke. But her heart was racing. It's just a game, she reminded herself, an erotic game. But oh, she thrilled to it.

'Sounds like fun,' she quipped.

His eyes flashed a stern rebuke at her. 'A sex slave is not concerned with her own fun. She exists just to give pleasure, not receive it.'

Charmaine pulled a face. 'Doesn't sound like a job that will catch on here in Australia. Except when the chap with the cheque-book has half a billion dollars to spare, of course. Although, if you recall, you only paid me for straight sex. So I reserve the right to object if things get too kinky. Meanwhile, would a slave really call you by your first name? I don't think so. How about just Master? That has a nicely submissive ring to it, don't you think?'

She scrambled off the bed and bowed with her hands together in front of her. 'I'll run ahead and run your bath, Master,' she said with mock-servitude.

'I *am* the master here,' he pronounced arrogantly.

'Only until I tell you the game is over,' she reminded him.

'Agreed,' came his smooth reply, but there was a devilish gleam in his black eyes. 'I must insist, however, that if you wish to quit you say so in advance, *before* the game has started in earnest. It is unfair to arouse a man, then leave him dangling.'

She laughed. 'I can't imagine you ever dangling.'

'That is just a figure of speech. So! Do you wish to continue being my sex slave?'

A quiver of nervous excitement fluttered in her stomach. Damn, but she could get addicted to this game. Dangerously addicted. Still, it was far less dangerous than the alternative—admitting that she did perhaps like Ali after all. No way was she about to do that!

'For tonight, anyway,' she said.

'Go run the bath, then,' he ordered. 'But no coloured additives or bubble bath. I wish to be able to see all of you in the water at all times.'

CHAPTER NINE

CHARMAINE often woke very early in the morning to a wave of emptiness, followed by the threat of depression. When that happened she would rise and exercise furiously till her dark mood passed, or was at least pushed aside for the moment.

That morning she woke not only very late, but also to a delicious feeling of peace, although she did experience a small knee-jerk of surprise once she realised she was back in the pretty pink bed. Ali must have carried her in there after she'd finally fallen asleep.

He hadn't stayed, however. He must have returned to his own quarters, and his own bed.

Charmaine quickly realised that waking up alone the morning after a night like last night was a definite plus. She could snuggle down under the duvet and think about all that had happened, without having to feel guilty or embarrassed, or whatever other awkward feelings might have consumed her if she'd woken still glued to Ali's naked body.

Don't think about Ali's naked body! came the immediate warning.

Too late. She was already thinking about it, and remembering. How it had looked and felt. How she'd been compelled to touch him all the time, and kiss him, and invite him back inside her, over and over and over.

Yet she didn't feel a bit sore this morning.

Obviously she'd been more than ready for him every single time.

Great sex, she finally decided after she'd wallowed for a while in her memories, had to be the best sleeping tablet in the world, plus the best anti-depressant. Once you were seriously turned on, making love was brilliantly mindless. And very morish. Once was never enough.

Fortunately, Ali was not a once-only man. He seemed to want her as much, if not more, than she wanted him. Of course, any man who'd paid five hundred million dollars for a woman had to be suffering from one huge dose of lust.

Even thinking about the money part didn't spoil Charmaine's feelings of delicious pleasure. Amazingly, she was beginning to find this whole scenario extremely satisfying indeed. All those lovely orgasms, plus all that lovely money. A girl such as herself would have to be mad not to be happy.

Or as happy as she was ever going to be. Charmaine did not delude herself into thinking that she would ever be really happy in life.

But things weren't too bad at the moment. She had five hundred million dollars to do good with. And a wickedly sexy sheikh at her disposal to be bad with.

The only problem she could foresee was Friday. Charmaine suspected that by then she might be somewhat addicted to Ali. Already she was looking forward to tonight. Would he want a rerun of the slave-girl act? She rather hoped he would. It was a good cover for her feelings, which could quite easily get out of hand if she wasn't careful. She still could not believe some of the things she'd willingly done last night.

It was obvious Ali preferred to be the boss when it came to lovemaking.

Charmaine shivered at the memory of all that he'd done to her last night. So many different positions. And so many different places, not just the bed.

Dinner in the sitting-room had been an education. Who would have thought food could be used as an aphrodisiac? Or that a dining table could become an instrument of erotic pleasure? Or was it erotic torture? The glass had felt very cold against her heated flesh.

But that had been only one of many highly imaginative interludes. Ali had come up with ways to have sex that she'd never dreamt of, but never anything she hadn't ultimately enjoyed, even if she was reduced to begging occasionally.

And didn't he like that!

Charmaine wasn't sure if Ali was a sadist at heart, or just getting even for her once having said no to him.

Saying no to him now—during sex, anyway—was no longer an option, not unless *she* was a masochist, which she wasn't. The irony of being turned on by a man like him did not elude Charmaine, but there was no point pretending. Sexually, she was putty in his hands.

Ali's boast about being an excellent lover had been an understatement. The man knew what he was doing. It was a shame that she had to give him up, come Friday.

Although, now that Charmaine came to think about it, there was no reason why she *had* to give him up after this arrangement ended. If he was willing—and she had every reason to think he would be—she could continue to see him. Ali had said he came to Sydney

every weekend to play poker and to go to the races. When she was in town, she could rendezvous with him in his hotel suite on a Saturday night after he returned from the races. They could enjoy each other at their leisure and in private, without having to make their affair public.

Of course, she would have to be *very* careful that the paparazzi didn't get wind of anything. She would hate for the world to think she was Prince Ali's latest plaything, bought and paid for at an auction no less!

Charmaine shuddered at what her mother would say, and think. She'd already questioned Charmaine closely over the phone last week after reading the Sunday newspaper article about some Arab prince paying millions to have dinner with her. She'd been concerned over Charmaine falling prey to some kind of obsessed admirer. An understandable concern, under the circumstances.

Fortunately, her mother had accepted her explanation that Ali was an oil-rich sheikh who used any excuse to give millions away to charity. She had admitted that yes, she *was* going to dinner with him but no, there was *nothing* going on between them, nor would there ever be.

Charmaine sighed. Her mother would not be happy if she ever found out her darling daughter had lied to her, or that she'd been carrying on with such a man. No, the risk of continuing this affair was just too great. She'd given her parents enough angst and pain in the past. To give them more was unconscionable. Come Friday, she would have to give Ali up. But till then…till then, she aimed to enjoy what he could deliver to the full. And then some!

The bedside telephone ringing put paid to any more

planning and plotting. Charmaine rolled over and frowned at the pink instrument for a few seconds. She'd left a message on her own answering machine at home saying she was out of town and out of reach for this whole week. Then she'd bravely left her mobile phone at home as well—turned off. Instinct had warned her in advance that, whatever happened this week, it would be wise for her to be incommunicado. Since no one knew she was here, then this could only be an in-house call. Ali, perhaps?

Charmaine was irritated by the wave of girlish pleasure that suddenly swept through her at this thought. The last thing she intended to do was to start acting like some infatuated schoolgirl around him. He was still the same man who'd paid five million to force her to have dinner with him and five hundred million to sleep with him. Just because she'd enjoyed sleeping with him didn't mean she had to *become* silly.

Scooping in a gathering breath, she expelled it noisily then snatched up the pink receiver.

'Yes?' she said rather sharply.

'Cleo here. I hope I didn't wake you?'

'No, no, not at all,' she replied, relieved in a way that it was the housekeeper. Relieved yet perversely disappointed at the same time. 'I was just thinking about getting up. I know it must be horribly late. What time is it?' Her watch was still in the bathroom, and there wasn't a clock in the room. But she could see through the French doors that the sun had been up for ages.

'Going on eleven.'

'*That* late!' The last time she'd looked at the time—via Ali's Rolex—it had been just after two a.m.

She'd fallen asleep soon after that. Which meant she'd been out of it for possibly eight or nine hours. A record for her. She was usually pushed to get four hours a night.

'Ali said not to disturb you,' Cleo informed her. 'He's only been up a couple of hours himself. Had a quick breakfast and took off to do the rounds of the stud. He'll be back for a proper lunch around one so I thought you might like to join him. I'll set something extra-nice up for you both by the pool. It's a lovely day outside.'

'That sounds marvellous. Thank you. I'll get up straight away.'

'How about I bring some coffee and croissants along to your room to tide you over till lunch? Or is that too fattening?'

'No. Sounds marvellous as well.'

'My, but you're easy to please. Ali's brought a few of your modelling compatriots home to stay over the years and I always found them on the snooty side. Feeding them was an especially big problem.'

'You won't have any trouble feeding me,' Charmaine replied whilst frowning over her negative reaction to Cleo's news that Ali seemed partial to models. The thought that she was just one in a long line of the breed to grace his bed piqued more than her pride, and firmed her resolve never to see him again after Friday.

'See you soon, then,' Cleo said brightly.

Cleo was at the door in less than ten minutes, Charmaine having only managed by then to go to the toilet, brush her teeth and pull on the pink towelling robe that was hanging on the back of her bathroom door. The only nightwear she'd brought with her was

the red set and another equally tarty black outfit, neither of which seemed suitable for greeting the housekeeper in.

'You were quick,' Charmaine said as she let the housekeeper in, trying not to look startled by the woman's colourful clothes. Canary-yellow Bermuda shorts, topped by a bright red and orange top that should have clashed with Cleo's red hair but somehow didn't.

'I'm a fast worker.' Cleo carried the breakfast tray across the room to the far corner, where two chairs sat on either side of a good-sized corner table.

'Did you and your husband enjoy the movie last night?' Charmaine asked as she followed her across the room and sat down in one of the chairs.

'What?' Cleo glanced up from where she'd started pouring the coffee. 'Oh, yes; yes, we did. Ali told you we were going, did he?'

'He mentioned it,' she said a bit abruptly, not happy with the reminder of Ali's threats about how she could scream all she liked and no one would come to help her.

But she hadn't screamed, had she? She doubted any of the women he'd had up here ever did, except in pleasure.

Charmaine found she didn't like thinking about Ali's other women.

'Do—er—all Ali's female guests sleep in here?'

Cleo smiled a knowing little smile. 'There's no need to be jealous. Ali hasn't brought any lady home here for ages. And none have ever stayed in here.'

'I'm not jealous,' Charmaine said, but far too defensively. 'Just curious.'

'No need to be ashamed of caring for Ali, either. He's a man worth caring for.'

Charmaine thought it wasn't the right moment to mention that she didn't care for the man. Not in the way Cleo meant.

'Really,' she said noncommittally, and picked up the first of the two scrumptious-looking croissants.

'People often misjudge Ali because he can be a bit stiff at times,' Cleo said as she poured Charmaine's coffee. 'You know, *royal*. But I can honestly say he's one of the nicest men I've ever met. Genuinely kind and compassionate. Cream and sugar?'

Charmaine nodded. 'Two cubes.' She figured she'd burned up more than enough calories last night to indulge herself today. She'd hardly touched the dinner in the end. Ali had eaten most of it, some off places on her body that in the cold light of day should have shocked her. It didn't, which was telling in itself, and reminded her of the type of man she was dealing with here. A rogue and a corrupter of women.

'And how is he kind and compassionate?' she asked, scepticism in her voice.

'Oh, countless ways. Take Jack for instance.'

'Jack?'

'The fellow who carried your luggage in last night. Jack's a cousin of mine. He's got special needs. No one would give him a job, but Ali did when I asked him. Like a flash. He's often given jobs to people who were down on their luck, especially married men with kiddies. Given them free accommodation, too. There's quite a few old cottages on this place. He's very good to everyone who works for him, provided they work hard in return. But he never expects anyone to do what he isn't prepared to do himself. The men

appreciate that. There's nothing Ali won't do. Muck out stables. Stay up all night with a mare in labour. Plough. Paint fences. Jack thinks he's just the ant's pants. And so does everyone else around here. You just ask them. No, perhaps that's not a good idea,' she added laughingly. 'I can see Ali being quite jealous if you started chatting away to the men. So just nod and smile when he shows you around the stud after lunch.'

'Do you think he'll do that today?' Charmaine asked, her mind still digesting Ali's glowing character reference. He was either a clever man, knowing how to get the best out of his staff, or he had a good side. Charmaine conceded no person was all black or white. She herself was no angel but she could be kind and generous to people less fortunate than herself.

'Oh, yes. He's terribly proud of this place. He's done wonders since he became manager.' Cleo placed the coffee-cup and saucer in front of Charmaine.

'Did he build this house?' Charmaine asked between mouthfuls of croissant.

'Heavens no, the manager before him did that. An Arab sheikh too, but nothing like Ali. A big, fat, lazy fellow. From what I've heard, he did nothing but spend the money on himself that should have been spent on buying decent stallions and mares. Actually, Ali doesn't care for this house much at all. Says it's way too large for his needs. It has twelve bedrooms, you know. Mostly we keep a lot of them shut up with dust covers on, but around Christmas I clean them all out and make up the beds with fresh linen and he lets any of the staff's relatives who want to visit stay here. It's bedlam, really, but wonderful. I love it.'

Surprise had stopped Charmaine's coffee-cup half-

way to her lips. 'But…but Muslims don't celebrate Christmas!'

'Ali lives by the credo of when in Rome do as the Romans do. I suppose one might call him a lapsed Muslim, in some ways. A lapsed prince when he's home here as well. Not that you can blame him. That lot over in Dubar never contact him for anything other than business. I throw him a birthday party every year and not once has he received a present, or a card, or even a phone call. Miserable lot! Who needs enemies when you have family like that? But I'd better not gossip about them,' she muttered. 'Ali wouldn't like it. He likes *you*, though, love. More than likes, I'd say. Have you known him long?'

Charmaine wondered what to say to this question. Clearly, Cleo didn't know anything about the auction or the dinner date Ali had won with her. She couldn't have read that article in the Sunday paper last week.

'We met at the Melbourne Cup carnival last year.'

'Goodness, *that* long ago. And he's only just brought you up here? Been playing hard to get, have you, love?' she said cheekily. 'Well, whatever, it's working. Never known a man so hyped up as he was last week. Then when he rang on Sunday to say he was bringing home a special guest and I was to get this particular room ready, I said to Norm that our Ali must have met someone really special, and when you turned up I knew I was right.'

'I'm not so very special,' Charmaine refuted, embarrassed by the housekeeper's compliments, plus her mistaken notion that Ali had been smitten by a once-in-a-lifetime love. 'People think fame makes you special but it doesn't.'

'Oh, I know that, love. I wasn't talking about your

fame. Or even about your beauty. I was talking about you. You're a real sweetie. And wonderfully down-to-earth. Just the sort of girl Ali needs to bring him out of that shell he goes into occasionally. Been extra bad this past year. But he was bright-eyed and bushy-tailed at breakfast this morning, I can tell you,' she said with a wickedly knowing gleam in her eye.

Charmaine was hard-pushed not to blush. The woman was incorrigible, but lovable at the same time.

'That's nice to hear,' she said.

Cleo laughed. 'You play your cards close to your chest, don't you, love? Smart girl. Look, I'll get Ali to come and collect you when he gets back. He's sure to want to shower and change before lunch.'

'No, I'd really rather not do that,' Charmaine said swiftly. 'I'd rather come and help you with the lunch. It won't take me more than half an hour to get ready, which means I'd just be sitting around in here, doing nothing.'

Cleo blinked in surprise. 'You really are a most unusual girl. But I won't say no to some help. Righto, when you're ready, just make your way to the kitchen.'

'You'd better give me directions. This house is huge. I'll probably get lost.'

'No, you won't. The house *is* big, but the floor plan is simple. It's shaped like a T. Go back along the corridor you came along last night till you get to the foyer, then turn left and go down that corridor. The kitchen is the second door on the right.'

'Well, that's straightforward.'

'One thing before I go. Please don't go making your bed. I have a girl who works for me who does that. She does all the washing and ironing as well.

She'll do your room and be along to empty your clothes basket whilst you're at lunch. She couldn't do it earlier because you were asleep.'

After Cleo left, Charmaine bolted down her coffee and croissants then set about getting herself ready in record time. Having declared she wasn't one of those vain pusses who spent hours on their appearance, she had to live up to the claim. But even the most minimal of self-care took time, especially when you had hair that fell to your waist. In the end, she plaited it whilst still wet then dressed in white stretch jeans and a simple white vest top that had no sleeves and a not-too-low V-neckline. In light of a possible tour around the stud after lunch, she chose comfy flat fawn loafers and kept her make-up to a dusting of blusher and coral lipstick. No perfume, either. She would save that for tonight.

Her trip to the kitchen was as direct and simple as Cleo had indicated. Once again, Charmaine spied little of the house on the way, although this time she took more note of the artwork that hung on the walls. No doubt original oils, they ranged from very modern to more traditional landscapes. Charmaine had an eye for art and was well-aware each one would have cost a small fortune.

The kitchen itself proved to be as large and well-equipped as one would expect in the home of royalty. It also had lovely large windows that overlooked a terracotta-tiled terrace and a huge swimming pool with water as blue as the sky above. At the far end of the pool stood a pavilion-style structure with three-hundred-and-sixty-degree views of the property, and it was in there, Cleo informed Charmaine, that lunch

was to be set up on a marble table fit for a prince and his lady-love.

Once again, Charmaine didn't bother denying that she was Ali's lady-love. No point. Cleo wouldn't believe her.

In the end, Charmaine didn't do very much of the food preparations, with Cleo only allowing her to do minimal fetching and carrying. Somehow—possibly by the sound of water running through pipes—Cleo knew the exact moment Ali arrived back, announcing that he would be along shortly, and she—Charmaine—should await him out by the pool. Cleo seemed to think he wouldn't be too thrilled with her playing maid.

Charmaine chose to wait for him at the table inside the pavilion rather than at one of the outdoor settings by the pool itself. When Ali made his appearance through the kitchen door a couple of minutes later, she was glad she'd made that choice.

Charmaine had often scorned women who said some man took their breath away. But as Ali stepped out onto the sun-drenched terrace, her own heartbeat stopped for a few drama-filled seconds.

The shadowed privacy—plus the distance from the house that the pavilion afforded her—gave Charmaine sufficient time to recover from the shock of her reaction. But her eyes continued to follow him slavishly as he made his way along the side of the pool, her mind revolving as it sought the reasons behind this most uncharacteristic response.

It couldn't be his handsome elegance which had sent her into temporary cardiac arrest. Ali had always been excessively good-looking. And a cool dresser. The denim shorts he was wearing looked great on

him, as did the sky-blue polo top. And, whilst some men looked ridiculous in sandals, he did not, perhaps because his feet were as brown as the rest of him.

She swallowed as she recalled again how magnificent his body looked naked. That had to be it, she decided with something like relief. It was lust which had made her heart stop, and more lust now making it pound.

She'd never been in lust before. Not really. That long-ago sexual attraction which had made her act so foolishly—and so disastrously—was nothing like this. This was on a different level entirely.

Thank goodness she now had the maturity and the character to handle her feelings, however primal and powerful they were. Charmaine wasn't ashamed of the way she'd acted last night, but she valued her composure at moments like this. She had no patience with females who ogled and drooled.

Of course, it would help if Ali didn't keep looking at her as if he'd prefer to have *her* for lunch, instead of the food on the table. Those hot black eyes of his seared over her face and body as he approached, telling her in no uncertain terms that any tour of the stud this afternoon was going to be brief.

Charmaine swallowed again.

'You slept well, I hear,' he said as he dragged a chair out at the table in the place opposite her.

'Very. And you?'

'The best I have in a year.'

His meaning did not escape her. He meant since he'd first set eyes on her. Charmaine tried not to let his flattery—or her own rapidly increasing lust—undermine her intention to have done with this affair, come Friday.

'So what would you like to do after lunch?' he asked as he selected one of the warm, crunchy bread rolls from the basket on the centre of the table and tore it in two.

Charmaine fought temptation with every shred of will-power she owned. As bold as she'd been last night, today was another day. And the situation was entirely different, especially now that she realised how weak she could be around him. She had to exercise some control over herself, or she might be in serious trouble. Men like Ali were fine to have a fling with, but not to become obsessed with, or, heaven help her, fall in love with.

As Rico had said, he could be dangerous.

'Cleo said you would like to take me for a tour of the stud,' she commented lightly, and occupied herself pouring a glass of mineral water from one of the chilled bottles on the table.

He smiled, a smile that carried a sip of cynicism and a large dose of devilry. 'And do you think that is how I would like to spend this afternoon with you?'

Her gaze met his squarely and coolly. 'I am certainly hoping you do,' she returned. 'Your insatiability last night has left me just a little...tender in places. I need a few more hours to recover before this evening.'

He laughed. '*My* insatiability. I seem to recall it was you who kept begging for more.'

She feigned a nonchalance she far from felt. 'Possibly I did. Once or twice. I have to admit you are very good in bed, Ali. You've certainly set a benchmark for the performances of my future lovers. I almost regret that this arrangement has to end.' She

noted the tightening in his facial muscles when she said this, but deliberately ignored it.

'Oh, and speaking of this arrangement,' she went on matter-of-factly, 'have you checked to see if the money was properly transferred to the foundation's account this morning?'

CHAPTER TEN

IN HINDSIGHT, Ali didn't know how he managed to hide his feelings at that moment.

Dismay was his first reaction to her monetary reminder. Followed by a crushing sense of his own stupidity.

Had he honestly begun to believe she felt something for him; that by the time he'd carried her back to her bed in the wee hours of the morning, she'd surrendered to more than the sexual chemistry that had always sizzled between them?

What a fool he was. A besotted fool. A *bewitched* fool. Yes, that was what he was. Bewitched. She had bewitched him from the first moment he laid eyes on her in that television commercial, then bewitched him further last night with her astonishingly sensual abandonment. When he thought of the way she'd moaned beneath his mouth, and trembled at his touch, and clung to him as she came...

But there was no glaze of desire in her eyes today. They were clear and cool and very much in control.

His gaze raked over her, taking in the virginal white clothes and schoolgirl plait which only emphasised the air of innocence that had always intrigued him and which this morning seemed to be especially mocking.

His dismay finally gave way to anger, his male ego smarting under the realisation that, regardless of how much delight she experienced in his arms, her priority

with him was always going to be that five hundred million dollars.

'It is all there,' he ground out, vowing to make her pay tonight for every single dollar.

Charmaine regretted her words the moment they were out of her mouth. She hadn't meant to sound so mercenary, or to make him angry. But for pity's sake, what did he expect? That she would *forget* that he'd virtually forced her to come here with him? Did he think she was going to let bygones be bygones and start playing the role of romantic lady-love for him?

OK, so they'd shared some amazing sex last night. And yes, he was one fabulous lover. But she had no intention of pretending that they shared anything more. For Cleo she might, yes, but not for him.

At the same time, she didn't want to spend the next four days in an atmosphere of open hostility. Ali in a bad mood was not fit for human consumption, let alone lovemaking. The one thing bound to turn her off was a lover whose passion was overlaid with anger. What she'd liked about last night was that, in the end, it had been such fun. Clearly, some compromise was called for.

'Look, I'm sorry,' she said, realising ruefully that there would be no smoothing over of things from Prince Ali of Dubar. She could tell by the set of his jaw and the cold fury in his black eyes that he'd just declared war on her again. 'I didn't mean to upset you, but I can't pretend that the foundation doesn't come first with me. That doesn't mean I didn't enjoy last night, or even that I'm not looking forward to a repeat performance. I'm even growing to like you...a little bit,' she added swiftly when his highly expressive eyes gleamed with satisfaction. 'Cleo has said

such nice things about you this morning that I can't continue to hold to the view that you're totally arrogant and spoiled. You do seem to have some redeeming qualities. Although the way you react to the word no is not one of your virtues. How many men do you think would go to the lengths you have to get a woman into your bed?'

'Not any woman,' he retorted. 'Just you, Charmaine.'

'Flattery won't get you anywhere with me, Your Highness. I think I told you that once before.'

'Ali,' he reminded her curtly.

'Ali,' she repeated with a sigh. 'See what I mean? You still must have things all your way.'

'We all like our own way. You do, too, Charmaine. But you might be surprised to discover that in my dealings with you I have not always given in to my desires. If I had been totally selfish, I would have had you during our helicopter ride here. I would not have waited. And if I was to yield to my dark side right now, it would not be this roll I would continue eating. I would sweep this table clear and spread you across its marble surface and feast myself on a far less dry food.'

The scenario he described brought a wave of heat washing through her body, burning its way up her neck and into her face.

'Would you let me, I wonder?' he asked her, his smouldering eyes locked to hers.

'No,' came her surprisingly firm reply.

'No…'

He smiled, then shrugged. 'See? I *can* take no for an answer. It will be the grand tour instead, in that

case, followed by a swim, if you would like. Would you like?'

'I...I can't really afford to be out in the sun long on days like this,' she said by way of an excuse, though privately thinking she wouldn't be able to keep her hands off him once he was half-naked. 'I might burn. Or tan unevenly, which doesn't look good either on the catwalk or in photographs.'

'I see. I had better use the golf-cart to show you around the property in that case. It has a roof. I was thinking of riding, but under the circumstances that can keep for another time. The swim as well. After the tour, I would suggest you lie down till dinner or have a long, leisurely bath. Speaking of dinner, I have decided we will dine in the main dining-room tonight. It will give you a little more time to be less...tender.'

'How kind of you,' she murmured, thinking what a wicked devil he was. But an entertaining one. 'Cleo tells me you're often kind. I heard what you did for Jack.'

He seemed embarrassed by this revelation, which endeared him to her more than anything else he had done so far. She respected people who did good work without wanting praise or publicity for it. A large number of the wealthy businessmen she canvassed for donations often wanted their so-called philanthropy to be widely known.

'It was little enough to do for someone less fortunate than myself,' he muttered. 'So what are *you* going to do with my five hundred million dollars? I hope you do not waste it on paying the exorbitant salaries of financial consultants. You should spend the money as *you* see fit. I am confident that you have your char-

ity's—and the children's—best interests at heart. Others might have more selfish and greedy agendas.'

'Don't worry. The money will be spent wisely and well. I won't fall into that trap. But I will take some advice from a few people whose business acumen I respect, then I'll get to work setting several projects in motion without delay. Time is of the essence when it comes to research, and in providing the right equipment and facilities to treat the poor little mites already afflicted. Trust me, I won't be letting grass grow under my feet. I'll be getting right on to things when I get back to Sydney. Fortunately, I have next week free of work, so I should be able to make some solid inroads during that time. I would also like to...'

Charmaine broke off her chatter and smiled. 'Sorry. Get me started on that subject and I never stop.'

'I really do not mind,' he said. 'I like to listen to a woman with passion in her voice.'

Charmaine swallowed, thinking he'd heard more than passion in the sounds she'd made last night. Each had had its own special message, from her gasps of startled pleasure to her groans of frustration, but the most obvious had been her cries of ecstatic release followed by her sighs of satisfaction.

'We should eat some of this delicious food Cleo's prepared,' she said, abruptly changing the subject from sex. 'Which reminds me—I really like your housekeeper, Ali. She's a lovely woman.'

'Yes. She is. I have become somewhat of a substitute son to her. She and Norman cannot have children.'

'Oh. Oh, how sad. She would have made a wonderful mother.'

'I agree.'

Charmaine didn't want to dwell on the subject of being a wonderful mother, either, so she started asking him about the stud. Being country born and bred, she wasn't totally ignorant of horses and surprised him, she thought, with her knowledge.

The lunch went well after that, and the tour of the stud afterwards even better. Charmaine couldn't help being impressed, both by the magnificent horses Ali owned and the amazingly modern amenities he'd had built to accommodate them. The breeding barn was something to behold, a huge structure with countless stalls, a very high insulated ceiling and a lovely wide breezeway through the middle to keep the inside at a pleasant temperature, even on the hottest summer's day.

The stud currently had six stallions on its books, Ali informed her, ranging from hopeful beginners to established top liners. One of these—a black named Ebony Boy—was breathtakingly beautiful, and an incorrigible show-off. When he was let out into his private yard for a spot of exercise, the stallion put on a real show, galloping around and kicking up his heels, as well as rearing up several times before pounding down onto all fours again and shaking his glorious mane.

'He's very spirited,' she commented. 'I'll bet he's hard to handle.'

'Not during the breeding season. But his book is winding down for this year and he is beginning to feel his oats once more. He is one of those stallions who is only content when he is covering several mares a day.'

Charmaine was taken aback. 'That seems excessive. Doesn't he ever get tired?'

'Of mating? Never.' And his eyes met hers, sending the same message to her about himself. If last night was anything to go by, then it was not an idle boast.

And yet...

'Cleo says I am the first female you have had up here for ages,' she remarked.

Ali scowled. 'Cleo's one flaw is that she is inclined to gossip.'

'Maybe, but she doesn't strike me as a liar.'

'I do go to Sydney every weekend, Charmaine,' he pointed out curtly. 'Trust me when I say that my carnal needs have always been well catered for. Do not imagine that I have been waiting for you to fall into my arms.'

Why did his remark hurt? It should not matter to her if he'd been sleeping with every second woman in Sydney. But strangely, she did feel hurt. And jealous. And downright snaky.

'If you had,' she snapped, 'you would have been waiting a long time.'

'I am well aware of that. Why do you think I took the extreme measures I did to achieve my goal?'

She turned to eye him rather coldly, as was her usual attitude when angry. 'And did you get your money's worth last night?'

His dark brows lifted in an attitude of total arrogance and nonchalance, both of which made her seethe. 'It was a reasonable return on my investment. But I aim to capitalise further tonight. And the next two nights. I would think that by Friday I will be well satisfied. But if not, I will make sure that the helicopter trip back to Sydney is much more eventful than the one up here.'

It was back. The hostility between them. And the tension. He claimed he liked to make love, not war, but with them there would never be one without the other.

'And that will be it?' she asked tartly.

'Are you saying you want an extension?'

'Never in a million years. Five days is what you paid for and that's all you'll be getting.'

He did not say a word in response to this. Just gave her one long, thoughtful look before turning to tell the groom to take the stallion inside again, leaving Charmaine with the awful feeling that she'd betrayed far too much. If this was war between them again, then she'd just made a tactical error.

Things said in anger—or fear—were always a mistake. She should have kept her cool, not jumped down his throat like that. No doubt he suspected now that he was getting to her; that underneath, she wanted more than Friday.

But suspicion was only suspicion, not fact. She would just have to pull herself together before tonight and show him that she wasn't total putty in his hands.

And just how are you going to do that? came the taunting question. How is this miracle going to be achieved? The man can turn you on with a look. If he touched you—even now, when you're as mad as a hatter—lord knows what you would still allow him to do.

You're trapped!

'Trapped' was not a state of mind to bring out the best in Charmaine. No man was ever going to trap her. She had vowed long ago to stay in total control of her life, and that included her sex life. That was why she'd sought out men she liked to go to bed with.

Because she refused to let one rotten, depraved bastard totally spoil that part of her life.

So stop waffling about *this* man, she lectured herself. You want him as your lover. You know you do. If you don't say as much then it will look as if he has won. You *will* fall into his arms whenever he wants. Is that what *you* want, to look a silly, weak fool in his eyes, to say one thing then do another?

Her small laugh got his attention.

'What is it that you find so amusing?' he ground out.

'You,' she answered. 'And me. We are both being silly here. But me especially. You are right, Ali. I do not want our affair to end, come Friday. That was my pride talking a moment ago. Plus some lingering anger over your bully-boy tactics. Oh, do not bother to open your royal mouth and deny it. You ruthlessly used your obscene wealth to come up with an offer you *knew* I could not refuse.'

'Sometimes a man has to do what a man has to do.'

Again, she laughed. 'Only a man like you. But that is water under the bridge now and it would be crazy of me to cling to my pride when you are as good in bed as you said you would be. Frankly, having discovered the delights of the flesh, I do not want to give them up yet. It worries me that I might not find another man who can meet my—er—special needs as well as you do. Clearly, I am not a girl who responds well to normal romancing. I seem to require a certain type of partner to turn me on. Someone very... masterful. If nothing else, you are that, Ali. Very... masterful.'

'Why is it, my dear Charmaine, that you can make a compliment sound like an insult?'

'Because beneath my sweet exterior, Ali, darling, I am a total bitch. Surely you must know that by now?'

He just stared at her.

'But back to the issue at hand. I am happy to continue being your lover after Friday, till one or both of us tires of the arrangement, that is. Not mistress, mind. Lover. I do not want a single thing more from you. No money. No gifts. Nothing, except that gorgeous body of yours, plus your titillating technique. *Comprenez-vous?*'

Again he did not speak a word, although his eyes spoke volumes. Dislike and desire darted across the distance between them like hot daggers.

'I thought I could come to you at your hotel suite each Saturday night,' she continued, determined to be pragmatic and not romantic. 'Except when I am overseas, of course. We could spend the night together, and Sunday, if you like. Are you happy with that arrangement?'

'Happy?' he echoed with a dry laugh. 'What is happy where you are concerned?'

'Oh, please, do not pretend I am the love of your life. We both know I'm not. I am an itch to be scratched. I am giving you the opportunity to scratch it. And before you ask, no, I will not be seen in public with you. That is my one firm rule. No dinner dates. No accompanying you to the races. Nothing but a sexual liaison. Agreed?'

For one awful moment, she thought he was going to reject her. Pay-back for what she'd done to him.

'And am I expected to be faithful to you?' he

asked, his voice as cold as his eyes had suddenly become.

What to say? *If you touch another woman, I will kill you* seemed over-the-top and very telling. But it was what she wanted to scream at him, what had burst forth from somewhere deep in her heart.

She had a ghastly feeling she had just made the biggest mistake of her life. But it was done now.

'That is your business,' she said offhandedly. 'I have no right to demand anything of you, as you have no right to demand anything of me.'

She could see that he didn't like her saying that. But that was too bad. He could damned well like it or lump it. The infernal man should have left her alone. But no, he had to have her, didn't he? Well, he could have her body but not her heart. Not to his knowledge, anyway.

'But if we promise exclusivity to each other,' he said whilst his eyes continued to shower her with fire and ice together, 'you could go on the Pill and we could enjoy each other more fully and more spontaneously without having to stop all the time to use protection.'

Little did he know but she was already on the Pill. One method of protection was never enough for Charmaine.

'Nature did not intend there to be anything between a man and a woman during the act of love,' he continued. 'Sensitivity is greatly enhanced by the feel of flesh sliding against flesh. The pleasure is far greater.'

Charmaine's head whirled at the promise of experiencing even greater pleasure than she had last night.

'Some women automatically come when they feel a man's seed flood their womb,' he murmured. 'They

say this type of orgasm is not only physically more intense but emotionally highly satisfying.'

If he'd thought that the image of his seed flooding her womb would make her melt, then he was sadly mistaken. It served to snap her out of her silly, almost-surrendered self and see him once again for what he was. A male predator who would use any weapon at his disposal to have what he'd always wanted, which was her as his sexual plaything, to be used without thought or care till he grew tired of her.

'I won't be going on the Pill,' she stated brusquely. 'And if you ever fail to use protection, Ali, I will *never* see you again.'

Shock flared in his face, followed by a studied thoughtfulness.

'I will do whatever you want,' he said at last.

'Good,' she snapped. 'In that case, I want to go back to the house now. I have a headache coming on.'

His eyes narrowed upon her. 'Is that the truth or an excuse to exit my company?'

'The absolute truth.' Little did he know it but he'd stirred up more than her hormones just now. He'd stirred up memories that were best forgotten, but which when remembered always made her blood pressure rise rapidly, resulting in the worst kind of headache. 'I suffer from migraines,' she told him, already seeing swirling flashes of light at the corners of her eyes, the precursor of the dreadful throbbing and nausea that would soon follow. 'I need to get to my pills quickly and lie down or tonight will be a non-event.'

'Come, then,' he said, and took her arm.

Charmaine wasn't sure if his solicitousness over the

next half-hour was out of kindness, or fear that she
would not grace his bed again that night. Whatever,
he whisked her back to the house and took her straight
to her room, where he himself pulled the curtains,
turned back her bed, fetched her a glass of water to
wash down her pills with, then saw her comfortably
settled before telling her that if the headache hadn't
totally gone by seven this evening he would cancel
dinner in the dining-room for that night. She could
have a tray in her room, or in his, if she felt well
enough. She only had to let him know. He would be
in his quarters next door. She only had to knock. Or
she could pick up the phone and ring Cleo if she
preferred.

'Just dial zero,' he told her on his way out, then
softly closed the door behind him.

Charmaine lay there underneath the pink sheet,
staring up at the canopy for ages, waiting for the dis-
comfort to start. But the throbbing in her head did not
eventuate. Neither did the nausea. It seemed the pills
had worked their magic in time. They also forced her
to relax, and with that relaxation came tears. Not tears
for what had happened in the past this time, but tears
for what was happening now, in the present.

What a mess!

But then she was always a mess, she accepted, deep
inside where all the bitter truths lay. Ali had asked if
her headache was an excuse to exit his company. She
hadn't thought so at the time but maybe it was, because as much as she pretended a non-emotional in-
volvement with him to his face she knew, in her heart,
that she *was* becoming involved. So involved that it
scared her silly.

Of all the men to start falling in love with!

'Oh, God,' she sobbed, and turned her head into the pillow, clutching it for dear life. Tears rolled down her cheeks and dripped from her nose, wetting the pillowcase through. But nothing could stop them. They rolled on and on till exhaustion finally overcame her and tipped her into the blessed oblivion of sleep.

In his quarters next door, Ali was sitting at his desk and frowning at the email from AIS. It was not a progress report but a request that he call the office personally. When he did, he was put straight through to the head of security, a man named Ryan Harris, whom he'd dealt with many times before.

'Glad you called, Your Highness,' Ryan said. 'I wanted to have a private chat with you concerning the in-depth background check we're conducting on your behalf on a certain lady. Pardon my being circumspect, but I think it best I not say her name. Phone lines are not always as secure as we would like, and e-mails, of course, are notoriously insecure.'

'I appreciate your care, Mr Harris,' Ali said. 'Having anyone investigated is always a sensitive issue. So what is it that you have found out?'

'A certain rumour has come to light during the past day, which, in view of the lady's high public profile, might present a problem if pursued further. Just asking questions, no matter how discreetly, can create a steamrolling effect where the rich and famous are concerned. I wanted to make sure you want us to continue.'

'What rumour are you referring to?' Ali asked with an instant tightening in his chest.

'One person in the lady's home town seems to

think that her younger sister—the one who died from cancer—was not, in fact, her sister, but her daughter.'

Shock at this news had Ali's hand gripping the receiver with white fingertips.

'How this has been kept secret is beyond me, given the fame of the person in question,' Harris went on. 'But I gather the community is close-knit, and my operative only gleaned this information via an off-the-cuff crack by a barmaid who works in the hotel there and who went to school with the lady in question. She might have been speaking out of jealousy or spite, but to dig further would be to give credence to the rumour and the gutter Press might get wind of it. They seem to have ears everywhere these days. I thought you might not want that, Your Highness, given your interest in the lady.'

'You are perfectly correct, Mr Harris. That is the last thing I would want. Please cancel the investigation immediately. And destroy the files in question. Naturally, the agreed fee still stands, as well as the bonus promised. I am most grateful for your discretion.'

Ali hung up and leant back into his desk chair, running his hands through his hair in agitation. Was it true? And, if so, when had the child been born and why had Charmaine denied her own daughter?

Shame?

She didn't seem like the type to be ashamed of being a single mother.

Ambition?

If she'd been that ambitious, why have the child in the first place? There were alternatives at her disposal.

A broken heart?

Now, that had the ring of truth about it. Being se-

duced, then later abandoned by a lover, explained Charmaine's actions and attitude to sex and men best of all. Love-turned-to-hatred-of-the-father could have resulted in her rejecting the child, although it did not condone such an action. Only the most hard-hearted or bitter woman, in Ali's opinion, would deny her own baby.

Of course, Charmaine *was* pretty tough. Tough *and* cynical.

Ali scowled and swivelled round in his office chair to face the window behind and the view beyond, a view that usually had the power to distract and soothe, especially when the sun was going down and the rolling hills took on that wonderfully warm glow. But his eyes did not see the glorious sunset at that moment. Or the splendid scenery. They were turned relentlessly inward, to his troubled thoughts and feelings.

How *could* he be in love with such a creature?

'Perverse,' he growled aloud, then grimaced.

Yes, such a love was perverse. He had imagined that knowing about her past would give him power over her. Instead, all it had done was make him sure he had no future with her, not the one he wanted, anyway.

She was good for one thing and one thing only. Foolish to fantasise anything else. She thought so too, having spelt out her intentions where he was concerned. The only role she wanted for him in her life was that of lover. Till she grew tired of him. She didn't even care if he was unfaithful to her. In fact, she *expected* him to be.

The realisation that she had such little regard and respect for him upset Ali more than anything else. She thought him a conscienceless womaniser, a man

who took women to his bed all the time without affection or caring.

The trouble was...she was right. That was exactly
what he had become over the past decade. A cold-
blooded user of women.

But his blood was not cold when dealing with this
woman. It was hot. Hotter than it had ever been before.

As for caring and affection...

Ali groaned. He did not *want* to be in love with
her. Given the circumstances, he would much rather
his feelings be confined to lust. Lust always passed.
But Ali knew he was already way beyond lust.

What to do to get her to at least agree to live with
him? He needed more of her than the occasional
Saturday night. What *could* he do to persuade her?

She would laugh at a declaration of love. Charm
and flattery had little to no effect. More bribing was
out of the question. He really had only one weapon
to use to get her to do what he wanted.

Ali's teeth clenched down hard in his jaw. It went
against the grain to use such tactics but she left him
no option. No option at all.

CHAPTER ELEVEN

'ARE you not glad that your headache is gone?' Ali murmured as he pushed aside her hair and bent his lips to her neck.

Charmaine shivered then turned her head to one side to give him better access. 'Mmm,' was all she could manage at the moment.

She was lying face down in the middle of his huge bed, dazed and dizzy with his lovemaking. His lips were working their way down her spine, licking and kissing her skin, his hands stroking her at the same time. His mouth lingered in the small of her back, whilst those oh, so wonderful hands slid between her legs.

She moaned, then whimpered with her rapidly escalating need to have him back where he had been just a few minutes before.

'Ali,' she choked out.

'What, my darling?'

She tensed at the endearment, or was it because his fingers had moved on to that spot which could not be ignored, or denied?

'Oh, yes. *Yes.*'

'Patience,' he exhorted softly. 'The time has not yet come.'

But she *was* going to come. Very soon. Her second climax since she'd presented herself at the connecting door to his suite an amazingly short time ago.

She'd woken from her sleep to find her room in

darkness and her head at peace. Not so her body. Within seconds, it was craving him. She'd tried a cold shower but that hadn't worked. The urgency of her need had driven her to don the pink towelling guest robe over her naked body and present herself at his door with not a scrap of make-up on, but her cheeks pink with desire. Or had it been shame?

One look into her eyes was all it had taken for him to know what she had come for.

He hadn't said a word, just swept her up into his arms and carried her into his bedroom once more. His eyes never left her as he'd laid her across the bed, parted the robe and then her legs, leaving her sprea-deagled like that, ordering her not to move whilst he stripped off and reached for protection. By the time he was ready, she'd been beyond ready.

She'd come within thirty seconds of his entering her. But he hadn't. He'd withdrawn then joined her on the bed, kissing and caressing her all the while. Now she was on the verge of coming again, trembling with need whilst he remained very much in control.

How did he do that? she wondered in bewilderment. Ignore his own arousal whilst she was off the planet?

He'd reached her behind by now and was rubbing his stubbly cheeks over her softly rounded ones. She moaned, her bottom automatically lifting off the mattress for more. When he stuffed a pillow under her stomach and pushed her thighs apart, she tensed in anticipation of his entering her. But no, he started rubbing his stubble over the soft skin of her inner thighs, at the same time blowing his hot breath against her wetness.

She whimpered in frustration and wriggled her bot-

tom. But still he did not give her what she desperately wanted. Instead, his mouth zeroed in, and her belly tightened further. His tongue swept down the valley of her desire and danced around her core. She squirmed and tried to hold on, squeezing everything tight to stop herself splintering apart. The waiting was cruel as he continued to tease and torment her. But then suddenly, blessedly, he was there, filling her, making her shudder with relief.

When he pulled her up onto all fours and cupped her breasts, she gasped with pleasure. He'd introduced her to this way of making love last night on the green carpet in the sitting-room. She had loved it then and she welcomed it even more now, partly because he couldn't see her eyes. He seemed to like to watch her face when she came and it worried her that he might see the increasingly emotional feelings that consumed her now each time his body joined her.

When he started pumping into her, she closed her eyes and tried to think of themselves as just two animals mating in the jungle somewhere. This wasn't about love. Just sex. Especially on his part. She had to keep remembering that.

His rhythm was punishing, his penetration deep, the grip on her both powerful and possessive. Gradually, she put aside all thought and let him take her to that brilliantly mindless place where she was reduced to primitive woman, free of all civilised concepts, free to mate like some wild animal in heat.

They made loud noises together, he grunting and she groaning. When she tensed then cried out in climax, Ali roared in reply. He arched backwards, pulling her upright and hard against him, his hands clamped over her breasts. Her mouth fell wide open

and she dragged in much-needed air, her mind whirling with the wildness of it all, her flesh squeezing then releasing him during seemingly endless contractions.

It felt an eternity before their mutual spasms ended and they fell back onto the bed, Ali rolling her onto her side, keeping her body moulded to his in the spoon position.

'Incredible,' he said softly into her ear. 'We are magic together, my darling. Magic.'

Charmaine was extra-glad that she couldn't look into his face at that moment, especially with tears suddenly stinging her eyes.

The telephone beside his bed ringing was not a welcome sound. Ali muttered something under his breath and Charmaine blinked madly in anticipation of his withdrawing. Terrified that he might roll her over and see her tears, she began to pull away from him herself.

'Do not move,' he barked, and, keeping one arm firmly around her waist, he reached over her and picked up the receiver.

With the phone only centimetres from her own ear, Charmaine could hear every word that was said. The trouble was the person on the other end was speaking in a foreign language, probably Arabic. Nevertheless, nothing could disguise the fact that the caller was a woman. When Ali exclaimed, 'Nadia?' in a shocked voice, Charmaine knew exactly who he was talking to. It was her, his brother's wife, the woman he loved, the married woman he'd been exiled over.

Dismay claimed Charmaine as she lay there, still fused with Ali's body and forced to listen to every emotion in his expressive voice. His surprise at hear-

ing from this Nadia. His concern over something. His soft words of comfort and caring.

The intimate-sounding chat went on and on, with Charmaine becoming increasingly distressed. How dared he make lovey-dovey small talk with this woman whilst he was inside *her*? How dared he?

When she made a further move to disengage their bodies, his arm clamped even more tightly around her, reminding her how strong he was. Too strong for her. Better she just lie quietly here till he was done. To struggle and to carry on would be very telling.

But the black jealousy that began to seethe through her was even more telling. To her.

She was not just *becoming* emotionally involved with Ali, she realised. She *was* involved. Hopelessly. Deeply. That was why she'd felt like crying just now. Because she knew that no matter how much Ali enjoyed making love to her, he did not love her; would *never* love her.

At last he was finished with the call. But it seemed he wasn't finished with *her*.

Not a word of explanation after he'd hung up. Nothing but a short, sharp silence before his attention snapped back to Charmaine's appalled body. Appalled, because she knew she still wanted him to continue, despite knowing his heart lay elsewhere and always would.

'Now, where was I?' he muttered, his hands stroking rather roughly up and down the front of her body. When they grazed over her bullet-tipped breasts, she shuddered convulsively.

Her disgusting vulnerability to him made her angry. And when Charmaine was angry she became very snaky, and stubborn.

'I thought I told you not to move,' he ground out.

'Go to hell,' she snapped. 'I'll move if I want to, whenever I want to. I am sick of you telling me not to move all the time.'

He sighed. 'You will never become really good in bed, my darling Charmaine, if you are not prepared to learn, or to practise control.'

'I am not, nor ever will be, your darling Charmaine.' She knew who his precious darling was. 'And maybe I'm not into control. Unlike yourself,' she added tartly.

'You think I want to control you?'

'Don't you?'

'I do not think any man could control you. Not totally. But it seems that the more control a woman practises over her public life, the more pleasure she often finds in abandoning all such control in the privacy of her bedroom. Is it not liberating to do as I say? To be mindless for once? To let someone else take responsibility for your pleasure, and your satisfaction? I am well equipped to give you both. But then, you know that is so. That is why you came to me tonight, and why you will continue to come to me from now on, whenever and wherever I want.'

'You wish,' she said, and laughed. But her laughter soon faded under the onslaught of sensation his hands began to create. The man must have sold his soul to the devil to know how to touch her like that, to make her crave like this.

She was desperate to move but refused to give in. She would show him that she could control herself, *and* resist him.

I will not move, she vowed frantically. I will not wriggle and writhe. I will not!

'You may move now,' he whispered after a few tortuous minutes. And with a tortured sob, she did.

CHAPTER TWELVE

ALI could not believe it when, shortly after the helicopter landed on the Regency rooftop that Friday, Charmaine refused to accompany him to his suite, telling him that she had wasted enough time that week. She said she had much to do with her foundation's new finances and would be in touch. She did not even leave him with her phone numbers or address, although he already knew both. She lived alone in a security-conscious apartment near Chatswood Station and had an unlisted number.

Pride, he decided after his anger had receded. Her damned pride. His pride then came into play too, because as much as he wanted her all that weekend he made no move to contact her, or force her hand in any way. He would wait for her to come to him.

And she would. He *knew* she would. No woman who had experienced what she had all week could indefinitely turn her back on such pleasure. Her body would eventually crave him again, as his craved hers. Sooner or later she would give in to that craving. He just had to be patient.

One week. One week since she'd seen him. One week of sheer hell, of sleepless nights and mental torment. She'd kept herself busy, working extremely long hours, having meetings with the people who could help put the foundation's incredible new bank balance

to work. Bank managers. Hospital administrators. Cancer specialists. Construction-company bosses.

By Friday, decisions had been made and put into action. There was to be a brand-new cancer wing at the children's hospital with a top-flight research unit included. The latest medical equipment was put on order from overseas and a real-estate agent had been commissioned to buy more homes near the hospital to provide accommodation for the families of the sick children, especially those who had to travel to Sydney from the country. Several new cars had also been bought and presented to the parents of patients who did not have a reliable vehicle for the extensive travelling often required with a sick child.

But by that same Friday, Charmaine found herself at breaking point where Ali was concerned. She had to go to him, even though she knew the time spent away from his corrupting presence was not nearly long enough. The sexual hold he had over her was even worse than she'd realised. Love made it worse. But denying herself his company, especially his love-making, had become unbearable.

So Charmaine booked a room at the Regency on the Friday morning for that night, a place in which to dress and to escape to if she needed a bolt-hole. Ali had mentioned to her the previous week during the helicopter ride back to Sydney that his friends arrived to play poker just before eight and didn't leave till after midnight. At the time, he'd obviously been expecting her to stay with him that night, a reasonable expectation, given she seemed to have lost all her will-power that week. She'd not only been at his sexual beck and call during the rest of her stay at the

stud, but had continued with her role of besotted bed-mate during the trip back to Sydney.

But the thought of his playing cards with Rico and Renée whilst she hid in his bedroom, waiting up for his return like some genuine sex slave, was beyond the pale. She could not do that to herself. And she hadn't.

She would not do it tonight, either. Hence her own room. But neither could she wait till after midnight. She needed to be with him, and soon!

Charmaine's telephone call, shortly after his arrival at his hotel suite, brought Ali great emotional relief, although nothing short of her presence in his bed would do anything for his physical frustration. Her abrupt announcement that she was actually in the hotel and would like to come up and see him for a short while before he settled down for his card-playing evening both excited and worried him. Did she mean what he thought she meant? He dared not ask. He might not like the answer. Just to see her was enough for the moment.

'I will have James organise a pass-key to be delivered to you,' he said.

'James?'

'The in-house butler.'

'Yes, do that,' she remarked drily. 'Then perhaps it would be wise to dispense with his services for a while. I wish to see you alone.'

Alone.

Was that good news or bad news? Ali's body hoped it would be good, since it had already leapt at the prospect of being with her again.

'I will dismiss him immediately.'

'I suspected you might.'

Cynicism in her voice. Naturally, she thought all he wanted from her was sex. He had to make her see this time that this was not so. He had missed her terribly, and not just her body.

She had garnered great respect from him when she'd actually left him last Friday. More so because he knew how hard it had been for her to do that. He had been merciless in his quest to bond her to him sexually that week, to programme her to do his bidding. He had used every seduction technique he knew. Every way of making her surrender herself totally to him.

But in the end she had still remained her own person. What courage she had. What character. What wonderful pride.

This last thought brought a moment of panic. Was she coming to see him to tell him to his face she did not want anything more to do with him?

Ali could not imagine what he might do if that was the case. Life, he had realised this last week, would not be worth living without her.

His mission impossible now was not to get her just to live with him, but to marry him.

By the time the doorbell rang ten minutes later, he was in a right royal state. It was an effort to relax his hands from the fierce fists they had become. The act of walking to the door and opening it was one of the hardest things he had ever done.

His breath exited his lungs in a slow stream of ill-concealed desire at the sight of her.

She looked breathtakingly beautiful, and wickedly sexy. There again, she *always* looked breathtakingly beautiful and wickedly sexy. But more so in what she

was wearing that evening, a pale blue silk slip-dress with tiny shoulder straps and a swishy skirt. Her legs, he noted, were bare of stockings and her feet were shod in silver sandals with heels high enough to bring her to eye level with him. Her hair was brushed back from her face but down, as he preferred it. Her face was quite heavily made up, her eyes surrounded by black eye-liner and smoky blue shadows, her full mouth made to look even fuller with a dark pink lip-stick. Silver drops hung from her ear-lobes. That perfume, which always drove him insane, wafted in merciless waves from her cleavage.

Impossible not to notice that she was bra-less, especially considering the erect state of her nipples. Impossible not to notice as well that *she* was looking at *him* with an almost shocking hunger, her eyes glittering as they raked over him from top to toe.

'Is he gone?' she demanded huskily. 'The butler—is he gone?'

He nodded. Difficult to speak. Her hunger had instantly become his hunger, bringing with it a fierce erection.

She stepped inside the foyer and shut the door behind her, her breathing shallow and rapid as she reached forward and pressed her right hand over his groin.

'Cruel,' she bit out.

He understood what she meant. It *was* cruel, the way they felt around each other.

Her fingers worked quickly on his clothes, freeing him to the suddenly cloying air in the foyer. Heat seemed to come from her in waves. Or was it him in danger of spontaneous combustion? For a split-

second, Ali thought she was going to kneel and take him into her mouth.

But she didn't. She just held his eyes whilst she pleated her skirt upwards with her hands, watching his stunned reaction to her nakedness underneath. When her dress was bunched at her waist she leant back against the door, bracing herself with her bottom and shoulders as she moved her legs apart.

'Do it to me,' she commanded, her breathing quickening further. 'No fancy foreplay. Just hard and fast sex.'

As brutally aroused as he was, Ali still recalled what she'd said if he ever made love to her without protection. Was this some kind of trap, a test, some twisted excuse for her to leave him?

'But what about pro—'

'I'm on the Pill,' she broke in brusquely. 'I have been all along. Don't look at me like that!' she snapped. 'It's what you always wanted, isn't it? To show me how incredible it is without anything between us? Do it, then. But do it quickly before I change my mind.'

He did it. Quickly. Roughly. Surging up into her again and again, glorying in her violent trembling, triumphant when her body came apart in his arms.

Now she was truly his, he thought with savage satisfaction as he came too, crying out his own raw release, unaware of the great gut-wrenching sobs which had overtaken her at some stage. It wasn't till his own cataclysmic orgasm began to pass that Ali realised something was wrong. Very, very wrong.

'Charmaine? Charmaine, darling, what is it?' He cupped her face with his hands but she just continued to weep hysterically. When her knees began to

buckle, he hoisted her up onto his hips and carried her into the bedroom.

His distress was as great as his confusion as he gently disengaged her from his body and laid her still shaking body on top of the blue quilt. When he pulled down her dress to a semblance of modesty, she sobbed and rolled away to curl into a foetal ball, her hands pressed under her neck, her eyes tightly shut. But even so, she kept on crying.

Ali didn't know what to do or to say to comfort her. Why was she weeping like this, as though her heart and soul were disintegrating? Hadn't he done what she wanted? Hadn't she enjoyed their mating?

Clearly not. Possibly, it *had* been a test and he had just failed it miserably. Whatever, he *felt* a failure. There he'd been, only minutes before, saying to himself that just seeing her would be enough. And what had he done? Taken her like some savage up against a door.

Self-disgust overtook him when he looked down at his own far from sated flesh. Stuffing it angrily back out of sight, he zipped up his trousers and climbed onto the bed behind her distressed figure.

'Hush, my love,' he murmured, and started to stroke her hair. 'You will make yourself ill.'

'You don't understand,' she choked out. 'I am being…punished.'

'Punished! How are you being punished? And for what?'

'The greatest sin of all.'

'Which is?'

'Being a bad mother. Oh, God, I didn't mean to tell you that. Now you'll despise me even more than you already do.'

'*Despise* you? Charmaine, darling, I *love* you. Surely you must know that by now.'

She froze, then slowly rolled over to glower up at him through soggy lashes. 'How dare you say that to me when you know I know it's not true? I was there, remember, when you took that phone-call from your true love? I *heard* you talking to Nadia. So warm and so loving.'

Ali winced in regret that he had not explained Nadia's call earlier. But he had been so angry with Charmaine at the time. And he honestly had not thought she cared. But now he saw how it must have looked to her and he was very sorry indeed. On the bright side, however, Charmaine's jealousy pointed to her having feelings for him that encompassed more than just lust.

He leant over her and pressed her back onto the pillow with a gentle kiss. 'Nadia is not my true love any more. I'm not sure she ever was. I did love her once. But it was the love of a spoiled young man who had always been given everything he wanted. I think not being able to have Nadia made my feelings for her seem stronger than they were. It wasn't till I fell in love with you that I realised what true love is all about. What you heard that night weren't words of love. Just caring and concern. Nadia called to tell me she had had cancer.'

'Cancer!'

'Yes. Cancer of the cervix. The doctors have cleared her, but facing the possibility of death, it seemed, made her see how much she really loved her husband, and vice versa. They talked together honestly for perhaps the first time in their marriage, telling each other of their true feelings. When she con-

fessed to Khaled about me, she was shocked to discover that he already knew about our forbidden romance and had been afraid all this time that she still loved me. When she reassured him that he was the only man she loved, he suggested she call me and clear the air. They were both worried that the reason I had not married was because of her. I was happy to tell her that I had met someone else, someone whom I loved and wanted to marry.'

'You want to *marry* me?'

'More than anything.'

'But…but you can't possibly. You don't really know me. I told you. I'm a bitch.'

'You mean because of this child you had? The one you were a bad mother to?' He had to be very careful not to betray his knowledge, to let her tell him everything in her own words and her own good time.

She nodded, tears filling her eyes again. 'Becky,' she said huskily. 'She…she died. Of leukaemia. She was only six and she…she never knew I was her mother. She thought I was her sister.'

At this she broke down again. Ali took her in his arms and just held her, till she finally stopped weeping.

'Sorry,' she muttered, drawing back to wipe her eyes with her hands. 'I…I don't like to talk about it. I get upset.'

'I think you should tell me about it, Charmaine. If we are going to be married there should not be any secrets between us.'

She stared at him again. 'You really mean it, about loving me and wanting to marry me? It…it isn't just a devious ploy to keep me sweet for some more sex?'

Ali had to smile. 'My dear Charmaine, do you

think after the way you acted when you came to see me tonight that I would have to lie to you to get more sex?'

She flushed. 'I...I don't know what's got into me. I've never been like this before. But then...I...I've never been in love before.'

Ali could hardly believe what he had just heard. He had hoped she might have fallen in love with him. But to hear the words...

'Not even with the father of your child?' he asked softly.

'With John? God, no. *No,*' she repeated with a shudder. 'I *was* very attracted to him, I admit. He was a little like you, actually. Very rich. Very handsome. Very suave. I met him when I first came to Sydney to do modelling. He was a good deal older than me. About thirty, I think. When he asked me out to dinner, I was flattered and excited. When he asked me to go back to his apartment for a nightcap afterwards, I foolishly went. I...I'd already had quite a bit to drink, and then I stupidly had another glass when I got to his place.'

Aha, so now he had some of the answers as to why she had been hostile to him to begin with. And why she no longer drank alcohol. He reminded her of this rich playboy who had seduced her, then abandoned her. 'The bastard took advantage of you whilst you were intoxicated.'

'No. Nothing as civilised as that,' she said with a cold little laugh, and his own blood ran to ice.

'He *raped* you?'

She nodded.

Ali sucked in sharply. 'I hope he is rotting in some

jail somewhere. Because if he is not, I will have to kill him.'

'He is already dead,' she said flatly. 'He died of a drug overdose a few years back.'

'Allah is just.'

'I actually don't remember the rape,' she said. 'He put something in the drink I had when I first arrived at his apartment. I remember feeling woozy and lying down on the sofa, then nothing till the next day. When I woke up, I was naked in his bed and I just knew he…he'd done things while I was unconscious. The trouble was I had no evidence of any assault. I wasn't bruised or bleeding in any way. I wasn't a virgin, you see. There'd been a boy at home. A…a neighbour's son whom I'd fooled around with the previous summer.'

Ali was taken aback by this admission. As much as he had always enjoyed the refreshing lack of sexual inhibition in Western women, he was sometimes still shocked by them. 'You were in love with this boy?' he asked carefully, trying to find some excuse for such behaviour.

'No,' she returned without a shred of guilt, or shame. 'We were just curious kids experimenting with each other. Things like that happen in the country, Ali. You have to be brought up there to understand. But it meant John had no trouble having sex with me. When I accused him of doing it to me whilst I was asleep, he freely admitted it. Then he told me not to bother to go to the police, that his father was a very important man and nothing would come of it. But I went anyway, more fool me.'

'What happened?'

'Oh, all the usual things. An embarrassing trip to

the hospital for tests and an internal examination. No evidence of rape there, unfortunately. Only lots of semen. And the blood test didn't show any drugs. By then whatever he'd given me was out of my system. When the police questioned him, he admitted having sex with me several times but claimed it was consensual. It didn't look good that I had gone to his apartment willingly, quite late at night. But his *coup de grâce* was the Polaroid photographs of me he'd taken.'

'Photographs,' Ali repeated, feeling sick to his stomach.

'Yes, he'd taken photographs of me, naked. In all sorts of lewd poses. Unfortunately, in some of them my eyes were half-open. I thought I definitely looked drugged and out of it. But the police said they looked like the glazed eyes of a turned-on girl during and after sex.'

Ali smothered a groan. As much as this whole scenario sickened him, he had to remember that she had had to live through it, then live with the consequences. His admiration of her courage grew, as did his sympathy for her plight.

'He told the police that I was an ambitious young model who had posed for the photos quite happily, but that I had turned nasty when he wanted to leave things at a one-night stand. His father called in some top lawyer to defend him and it wasn't long before all charges were dropped and I was left holding the baby, so to speak.'

'I do not wish to be insensitive here, Charmaine, but under the circumstances, why did you not consider a termination?'

'I went into denial. Refused to believe I was even

pregnant. It wasn't till I lost a modelling assignment because I was putting on so much weight that I was forced to face reality. I told my agent I was sick and went home to my parents. By then I was almost five months gone. I...I had some kind of nervous breakdown and demanded the baby be adopted.'

'You poor darling,' Ali said, and reached to touch her. But she shrank back from his hand, her eyes focusing blankly on some spot on the ceiling.

'Mum could see that I couldn't cope at that time but she thought that eventually I would regret having given up my baby. She came up with the plan to tell everyone it was *her* baby. We lived on an isolated farm, so it was easy for me to have the baby there at home without anyone knowing. No one even knew I was at home at that stage. All the locals thought I was still in Sydney. Mum just started putting some padding under her dresses and telling everyone she was expecting. I slept in my room most of the time, only too happy to have someone else solve my problem.'

Her eyes lifted at last to look at him. Such sad eyes.

'I know you must be thinking it was wicked of me to reject my own child,' she said brokenly, 'but I just couldn't look at the baby and not think about what John had done to me. After the birth, I...I couldn't get away quickly enough. By then I'd changed into a cynical, cold-blooded, truly ambitious bitch, determined not to let what one man had done spoil my life. I was still young and I vowed to be a success, not just as a model but in every area of my life. So I took a lover. He was a very sweet boy, but perhaps a little too sweet. Or too inexperienced. I rapidly moved on from one boyfriend to another, desperate to prove I wasn't frigid. But nothing seemed to work.

In the end I gave up men and sex, and just concentrated on my career.'

'So when did you begin to regret giving up your child, and motherhood?'

'It happened gradually, I suppose. Every time I went home, I would see Becky growing into such a lovely child. So outgoing and intelligent. It was worrying at first the way she gravitated towards me, the way she ran to me whenever I visited. But after a while, I thrilled to her open affection. I guess I also spoiled her, especially on her birthday and at Christmas. I bought her outrageously expensive presents. Compensating, I guess. Mum and Dad adored her and I kept telling myself I had done the right thing by Becky.'

Her sigh carried enormous regret and sadness. 'I didn't realise just how much I loved Becky, and what I had missed out on, till she was diagnosed with leukaemia. I'll never forget that phone call when Mum told me the news. It was like...'

She broke off and closed her eyes for a second before opening them and throwing Ali the most heart-rending look.

'I...I can't describe it. Anyway, we tried everything but nothing worked,' she went on in an artificially matter-of-fact voice. 'She had some rare form of the disease which didn't respond to a bone-marrow transplant. Chemotherapy put her into remission for a short while but then it came back, stronger than ever.'

Again she broke off, and just lay there, silent and sad for a few moments.

'It almost killed me to watch her die like that,' she resumed softly. 'It almost killed Mum, too. But at least she had the joy of being called Mum by my little

girl. Those last days…when we knew there was no
hope, I…I wanted to tell Becky. I wanted to hold her
and say, I am your mummy, darling, not your sister.
But that seemed cruel and selfish. So I kept my silence. I kept my silence and she died in my mother's
arms, not mine, and I… Oh, God, Ali…' Her eyes
flooded as she turned them despairingly to his. 'Hold
me. Just hold me.'

He held her and she just cried and cried. Ali vowed
then and there that somehow he would make things
right for this beautiful woman he loved. Somehow,
he would make her happy again. Somehow…

CHAPTER THIRTEEN

CHARMAINE lay back in the deep bath Ali had run for her, still amazed at how wonderful he had been. Not shocked by her confessions, or in any way judgemental. Just sympathetic and kind and so very understanding.

Maybe he does truly love you.

Charmaine smiled to herself at the maybe. What did it take to convince her, for pity's sake? The man had paid five million dollars to have dinner with her and five hundred million to sleep with her. Lust alone did not explain such extraordinary extravagances.

But possibly the most loving thing Ali had done for her so far was what he was doing at that moment. He was out there cancelling his Friday-night poker game so that he could spend the evening with her. How romantic was that!

Rico turned to Renée after putting down his phone.

'Ali just cancelled cards for tonight,' he said, his tone amazed.

Renée blinked. 'Good lord. That's a first. Why?'

'You know Ali. He didn't really explain. A personal emergency, he said.'

'Some woman, probably,' Renée surmised.

'He's never cancelled before.'

'Maybe he's finally met a woman who's made him forget that one back in Dubar you told me about.'

'I wonder…'

'Rico, what are you thinking?'

'Remember how you mentioned you couldn't contact Charmaine the week before last, that she'd gone out of town you knew not where? And when she came back and finally answered her phone, she was evasive over where she'd been.'

'You don't think…'

'*Sì*. I *do* think.'

'No!'

'Ali is not a man who recognises that word,' Rico said drily.

'Ali is also not Charmaine's type. He's far too macho a man. She'd run a mile.'

'Shall we bet on it?'

Renée smiled. 'You'll lose.'

'I bet he shows up at the races with her tomorrow.'

'Wow, that's some crazy bet! What stakes are we betting for?'

'The right to name our babies.' They had been arguing over that for days. Renée wanted Australian names whilst he wanted traditionally Italian.

'Done!' Renée said, supremely confident in winning.

Rico smiled, whereupon Renée looked worried.

'Is there anything you know that I don't know?'

'Absolutely not.' But Rico had not forgotten the way Charmaine had talked about Ali the night of the auction. If you simply disliked someone, you didn't bother with that kind of passion.

'One small problem, though,' Renée said with a sigh. 'I'm not sure I'll be making the races myself tomorrow. I'm feeling a bit funny in the tummy.'

'That's just the pickles and pizza you ate today. You know, if you keep giving in to all these cravings,

darling, you're going to be as big as a bus by the time you have those babies. You've still got a month to go.'

'I know. I've really ballooned out over the last couple of weeks. I look disgusting. I don't think I've even got a dress big enough to wear tomorrow.'

'You'll find something. I know you. You won't want to miss both cards *and* the races in one weekend.'

'You could be right. We are all slaves to our passions, aren't we?'

Rico didn't think she could have said a truer word.

When Charmaine emerged from the bathroom, the master bedroom was empty. Sashing the thick white hotel robe tightly around her, she went in search of Ali, and found him wheeling an elegant traymobile across the sitting-room. He stopped on seeing her, his black eyes looking her up and down.

'I am relieved that you did not put that blue dress back on again,' he said. 'That robe is much better for what I had in mind.'

Charmaine's eyebrows arched. 'And what exactly, Your Highness, did you have in mind?'

He smiled a wry smile. 'Not that.'

'Oh.' Was she surprised or disappointed?

'I would like us to start over and get to know each other a bit better before we make love again. It is very easy to be distracted by matters of the flesh. So I thought that for this evening we would sit out on the terrace and just eat and talk.'

Although knowing she would probably be frustrated as hell by the time the evening was out,

Charmaine had to agree with him. 'Good idea. Oh, and Ali...'

'Yes?'

'I know I said I loved you and I do. But please... don't try to rush me into marriage. I'm not at all sure that marriage between us would ever work.'

Ali refused to panic. It was only natural that she would be cautious.

'I think I know you well enough, Charmaine, to realise you would not be rushed into anything against your will. But I also want you to know that I believe marriage between us would work wonderfully.'

'But...but what about children?'

'What about children?'

'I...I'm not sure I want to have any.'

Ali's heart sank but he kept his cool. 'And why is that, my love?' he asked gently. 'Is it because of your past, or your career, perhaps?'

'My career! I don't give a damn about my career. Modelling has become just a means to an end for me over the last couple of years. It was the money I wanted, not the attention or the fame. I couldn't care less if I never set foot on a catwalk again.'

Ali was very pleased to hear that. 'When you marry me, you won't have to,' he told her. 'You will have all the money you need.'

'I would still want to be hands-on with my foundation.'

'Of course.'

'Would you marry me even if I said I would never have children?'

'Yes.'

'Just like that. Yes.'

'Yes.'

'Oh, Ali...' She came forward and reached out to lay a tender hand against his cheek. 'What a wonderful fool you are. But I do so love you. *Too* much.'

'There is no such thing as too much love,' Ali said, struggling not to forget his plans for a platonic evening and just sweep her into his arms once more.

'You do realise we won't last even one night,' Charmaine murmured, gazing deep into his eyes.

'Yes,' he said with a resigned sigh.

'But we can try,' she added, and dropped her hand away from his face.

Ali actually trembled with relief.

'Do you want me to help you with the food?' she asked.

'No. I want you to go out onto the terrace, sit down and keep your hands to yourself.'

Her laughter carried delight. 'I was getting to you, was I?'

He scowled. 'You will be made to suffer for your many transgressions.'

'Aah, promises, promises,' she countered saucily and sashayed out onto the terrace.

Ali followed in her wake, pushing the traymobile with white-knuckled hands whilst his dark side plotted all sorts of erotic revenge.

CHAPTER FOURTEEN

'WELL, you were right,' Renée sighed, still not totally recovered from the shock of seeing Ali arrive at the races with a glowing Charmaine on his arm.

'Of course I was right,' Rico replied smugly. 'Now I can name my daughter Angelina, and my son Alphonso.'

Renée shrugged. 'OK. Angie and Alfie it is.'

Rico looked appalled. 'Their names are not to be shortened like that. What is the point of giving proud Italian names if you turn them into English nicknames?'

'Rico, might I remind you that no one calls you Enrico except Ali. This is Australia. If your name is more than two syllables you haven't got a chance of keeping it once you hit school. So get used to having your children called Angie and Alfie. Or Ange and Alf.'

'Even worse!'

'Well, you could always let me have my way and give them good Aussie names to begin with like Lisa and Luke. No shortening to be done there!'

Rico growled under his breath. '*You* lost the bet. *I* get to name the children.'

'Whilst I get to go to the loo again,' Renée said with another sigh, levering herself up out of her seat in the stand. 'How long is it till the next race?'

'Four minutes. Maybe you'd better wait till afterwards.'

'Can't. I'm desperate.'

When Rico stood up and took his wife's elbow she told him, 'No, don't worry. I can go on my own.'

'Are you sure?'

'I'll get Charmaine to come with me. If I can pry her away from lover-boy, that is,' she added under her breath. 'Do you see the way she's looking at him, Rico?'

'Mmm. Sure do. I'd like to be a fly on the wall in *their* bedroom.'

'You might get your wings singed.'

'More likely burnt right off, I'd say. Not that we can talk. We've made a few fires in our day, haven't we, darling?' And he gave Renée a loving squeeze. 'I dare say we'll make a few more, once you pop those babies out.'

'I dare say, Casanova. Meanwhile, I really must... Oh. Oh, my God!' And she stared down in horror at the floor between her legs.

Rico thought she'd wet herself for a moment, but then he realised what had happened. Only last night, he'd been reading one of the several books on childbirth he'd bought and which listed all the ways labour started.

Rico had wanted to be well prepared for every eventuality. After all, with Renée expecting twins, it was highly likely the babies might want to arrive before full term.

He'd been so calm reading about it. Now, staring down at the puddle of water, panic was only a heart-beat away.

'We...we have to get you to the hospital as soon as possible,' he gabbled. 'That's what the book said.

Even if you haven't got any contractions. Have you got any contractions?'

'No. I mean…I have had this sort of backache on and off all day.'

'Why didn't you tell me? Backache is often the first sign of labour.'

'Rico,' she said wearily, 'I have had an aching back on and off for weeks. How would I have known the difference? Please let's not argue. Let's just go call a taxi.'

'Yes, yes, a taxi. I don't think I should drive. I feel a bit rattled.'

'How could you drive, anyway, when we didn't bring a car? We caught a taxi here, remember? But I will still have to go home first and collect my bag.'

'What's wrong?'

They both whirled to find Ali standing there, Charmaine with him, both of them looking anxiously at the puddle on the floor.

'My waters have broken,' Renée explained, holding on to her swollen belly for dear life.

'She has to get to hospital as soon as possible,' Rico jumped in, feeling more nauseous by the minute.

'We came in a limousine,' Ali informed them. 'I will instruct my security man to call the chauffeur and have him bring the car round to the main gate immediately. Can you walk that far, Renée?'

'Yes. I'm only leaking, Ali, not dying.'

'I'll carry her,' Rico said, which brought an exasperated glance from Renée.

'Don't be ridiculous, Rico. I weigh a ton. Just hold my arm and let's go.'

'She's still got a month to go,' Charmaine whispered to Ali as they followed Rico and Renée through

the crowd. 'I hope the babies will be all right.
Renée'll die if anything goes wrong.'

'She will be fine,' Ali replied reassuringly. 'The
babies will be fine.'

Charmaine wished she could be so confident. Life
was not always fine, or fair. Just because Renée desperately wanted these babies didn't mean everything
had to go right.

Fortunately, the limousine was there waiting when
they reached the gate and the exclusive private hospital Renée was booked into was only a short drive
away. Once they reached the hospital, Renée was
popped into a wheelchair and whisked away with
Rico to the maternity ward whilst Ali and Charmaine
were given the job of driving further into the city to
their penthouse and returning with the bag Renée had
already packed and which was sitting in the foyer coat
cupboard.

By the time they returned to the hospital and found
the right wing and the right sister to make suitable
enquiries to, Charmaine was amazed to be briskly told
that, 'Mrs Mandretti's labour has progressed rapidly,
she is fully dilated, the doctor has been called and all
is ready for an imminent birth.'

'But what about the babies?' Charmaine asked
worriedly. 'Will they be all right? They're early.'

'All their vital signs are good. Look, they have the
best doctor, the best midwifery nurses and the best
medical equipment money can buy,' the sister said
briskly. 'They will be fine.'

'I told you so,' Ali said as he led Charmaine away
to the waiting-room. 'Stop worrying. You will make
yourself ill.'

Charmaine *felt* ill. Her heart was racing madly and

her head had a vice around it which was gradually being tightened by some unseen torturer.

'I could never do this,' she muttered. 'Never.'

Ali knew what she meant. She could never have a baby. Never have *his* baby. His heart ached with the loss of what would have been a great joy to him. But nothing would change his mind about marrying this woman.

He sat down on an empty chair and watched her anxiously pace the room, her eyes continuously darting towards the wall clock. Ali wished there was something he could do to ease her anxiety, but he knew nothing but good news would achieve this goal. Time passed with agonising slowness, his own eyes checking the time every once in a while. About forty-five minutes after they had arrived, the sister they'd been talking to earlier suddenly popped her head round the door, all smiles.

'The babies have arrived. Both healthy and quite large for thirty-two weeks. The boy weighed just under three kilos and the girl two and half. They don't even need humidicribs. Both parents survived the ordeal, although I'm told the father had a few sticky moments. He's fine now, though. Proud as a peacock. The mother said to ask you to come in, and to bring her bag. She said she wants to have a shower and wash her hair. I'll show you the way...'

Tears flooded Charmaine's eyes as a smiling Ali took her arm. 'I told you everything would be fine.'

'Yes, you did,' she said, dabbing at her eyes with a tissue from her handbag. 'I'll take notice of you next time.'

Charmaine thought Renée looked remarkably well for a woman who'd just given birth. And blindingly

happy. Rico wasn't far behind in the happiness stakes, beaming like a Cheshire cat as he called his mother on his cellphone to tell her their good news. Charmaine could hear the Italian woman's excitement from across the room.

But it was the babies Charmaine could not take her eyes off, both wrapped up tightly and sleeping in their cribs beside Renée's bed. They had masses of black hair and weren't all red and wrinkly as Charmaine imagined even slightly premature babies would look.

'Oh, Renée,' she said as she walked over and stared admiringly down at them. 'They're so beautiful.'

'Indeed,' Ali agreed, having come over for a look as well.

'Would you like to nurse them?' Renée suggested generously. 'Charmaine, you take Lisa there. And Ali, you can pick up Luke.'

Ali didn't hesitate, scooping up the boy baby with surprisingly confident hands and rocking him back and forth like an old hand at it. Charmaine froze, suddenly stricken with the memory that not once had she held her own baby girl at this age. She'd refused to set eyes on Becky till she was six months old.

'I don't think I can,' she said, consumed with regret and guilt, but at the same time the most terrible yearning. 'I...I might drop her.'

'No,' Ali said, 'you won't.' And, handing Luke to his mother, he scooped up the baby in the pink bunny blanket and placed her in Charmaine's arms.

Little Lisa woke, and started to cry, her hands finding their way free and flapping around.

For a second, Charmaine froze further. But then automatically—no, *instinctively*—she took both of the tiny hands within her own firm grasp and held them

still as she settled the baby girl into the crook of her arm, then rocked and sang to her till she drifted off to sleep again.

'You're really good at that,' Renée praised. 'I might have to hire you as chief babysitter.'

'Any time,' Charmaine said huskily, then glanced up through shimmering eyes to smile at Ali.

His heart caught. Did she mean what he thought she meant? Was it possible?

Not a word did he dare say on the matter either during their visit at the hospital, or on the rather silent drive back to the hotel. If she had changed her mind about having a baby, then it had to come from her own lips. He would not try to pressure. Or persuade.

She didn't say much about anything, actually, not till after they'd made love that night and she was wrapped tightly in his arms.

'Ali,' she began.

'Mmm.'

'You know I have to go to Italy next week for a photo shoot. I've signed a contract so I really can't get out of it without the possibility of being sued.'

'Yes, I understand.'

'Then I have a few more modelling commitments I have to honour before the end of the year. There's fashion week in Melbourne, and after that I have to do another perfume ad for Femme Fatale.'

'You must do what you must do.'

'Yes, I must. I'd like to cut down on my modelling come the new year, however, and move in with you. Is that all right?'

'I would prefer us to be married.'

He felt her smile. 'I knew you were going to say that. In that case, a New Year wedding it will be. We

could have it at your property. An outdoor ceremony. Either around the pool or in the pavilion. But nothing too grand. And please, not too many guests. Just close family and friends. Cleo could do the catering for the reception.'

'Sounds perfect. But for a lady who did not want to be rushed, that does seem a little quick.'

'I want to make sure I don't look fat in the photos.'

'What do you mean? You would never look fat.'

'I will when I'm pregnant.'

Ali stopped breathing.

'I'm going to stop taking the Pill tomorrow, if it's all right with you.'

He began breathing again. 'Perfectly all right.'

'I realised tonight that I *do* want a baby, Ali. And this time, I think I might make a pretty good mother.'

'You will make the best mother.'

'I don't know about that. But I'd like to give it a try.'

Ali's arms closed more tightly around her, his lips in her hair. 'You have made me the happiest man in the world.'

'Happier than Rico?'

'Enrico is a very lucky man. But I am luckier. I have you.'

'Oh, Ali…I think I am the lucky one to have you.'

'We are both lucky.'

'Yes,' she said, and sighed with happiness. 'Yes, we certainly are.'

EPILOGUE

Christmas Day the following year

'WHOSE idea was it,' Charmaine said to Ali as she dashed into the bathroom to do her hair, 'to have absolutely everyone come to our place for Christmas this year?'

'Yours,' Ali said to her reflection in the mirror, and calmly continued shaving.

Charmaine picked up a hairbrush. 'You could have said no.'

'I never say no to you, my darling. You know that. But what is worrying you? Everything is organised. Cleo told me less than half an hour ago that all the women had helped her get the food ready and there was nothing left to do except get cleaned up and dressed.'

'Yes, Renée and Dominique have been marvellous all morning. And Rico and Charles have been doing their childminding bit. I guess I'm just in a bit of a tizz because Mum and Dad are here. They make me nervous after the way they reacted to our marriage. I mean…they weren't exactly thrilled, were they?'

'It is understandable that they were wary of me at first. But by the time Amanda was born, they believed my intentions towards their daughter were honourable.'

'Yes. You're right. They adore you now. And they

182

adore Amanda. But then, she is just so adorable. Only five months old and already a heartbreaker in the looks department.'

'Must take after her mother,' Ali murmured as he tipped his head back to shave under his chin.

Charmaine laughed. 'You know very well, you arrogant devil, that there's hardly a scrap of me in her. She's you through and through. It seems you're one of those pre-potent sires.'

Ali stopped shaving, his eyes whipping round to stare at her with surprise. 'You have been reading my books on breeding horses.'

Her shrug was light. But inside, she was far from nonchalant. It wasn't her parents' presence so much making her nervous, but the news she had to tell him.

'I—er—I thought if I was going to be a stay-at-home mum, I would have to get interested in something. So I've decided to educate myself on the main topic of conversation around this place. On top of that, Cleo promised to teach me loads of card games for us to play together.'

'But that is wonderful!' Ali exclaimed.

'I'm glad you're pleased. Hopefully, you'll also be pleased with my other Christmas present.'

His dark brows drew together. 'Another Christmas present? But you have already given me a digital camera and the lovely clothes I will be wearing today. What else have you bought me?'

'It is not a present that can be bought, Ali.'

'Really? What, then?'

'I...I'm pretty sure I'm pregnant again. We're going to have another baby.'

'But I thought you could not conceive whilst you were breastfeeding.'

'It's not a sure-fire method of contraception. And Amanda's not having as much breast milk now that she's on solids. I haven't been to the doctor yet but my period is over a week late and the three home tests I used this week all turned blue.'

Ali put down his razor and reached out to take her into his arms. 'Another child,' he said. 'Now, that is the best Christmas present of all.'

'Maybe we will have a boy this time.'

'It does not matter. I would be just as happy with another girl.'

'But I thought...'

'You think too much sometimes.'

Charmaine sighed her relief. She'd been a bit worried that Ali might think it was too soon for her to have another baby. Or that he was set on having a boy. She wasn't all that keen on men—or cultures—who valued boy babies over girl babies.

'I would like a dozen children,' he said. 'And it would not matter if they were all girls. We are living in Australia, Charmaine, not Arabia.'

'But what about in your heart? Is a baby girl as important as a boy there?'

'How can you ask such a thing when my heart has already been captivated by the most beautiful girl in the world?'

'Oh...'

He took her chin with his fingers and gave it an affectionate squeeze. 'Come, do not cry.'

'I am crying with happiness.'

'Is that the truth? You are really, truly happy?'

'I never knew you could be this happy.'

Ali almost cried himself. 'I am going to kiss you

now. But only once. You know what happens if I kiss you twice.'

He kissed her. Then he kissed her again.

They were only a little late for dinner.

Modern Romance™
...seduction and
passion guaranteed

Tender Romance™
...love affairs that
last a lifetime

Medical Romance™
...medical drama
on the pulse

Historical Romance™
...rich, vivid and
passionate

Sensual Romance™
...sassy, sexy and
seductive

Blaze Romance™
...the temperature's
rising

27 new titles every month.

Live the emotion

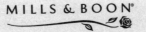

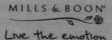

MILLS & BOON®

Live the emotion

Modern Romance™

THE BANKER'S CONVENIENT WIFE by Lynne Graham

Italian-Swiss banker Roel Sabatino has amnesia and is feeling a little confused – he has a wife whom he cannot remember marrying! Hilary is pretty, sweet...and ordinary. But Roel still recognises a deal when he sees one and decides to enjoy all the pleasures marriage has to offer...

THE RODRIGUES PREGNANCY by Anne Mather

Olivia Mora didn't expect that one night of passion with handsome South American businessman Christian Rodrigues would lead to so much trouble! Determined to keep her pregnancy a secret, she retreats to a secluded tropical island. But Christian is a man who doesn't give up easily...

THE DESERT PRINCE'S MISTRESS by Sharon Kendrick

Multimillionaire Darian Wildman made an instant decision about Lara Black – he had to have her! Their attraction was scorching, and desire took over. Then Darian made a discovery that would change both their lives. He was the illegitimate heir to a desert kingdom – and a prince!

THE UNWILLING MISTRESS by Carole Mortimer

March Calendar is sexy, single – and she wants it to stay that way! Will Davenport might be the most eligible bachelor she has ever known, but he's also the most lethal. But from their first fiery meeting Will has been hooked on March – he wants her and will do anything to make her his...

On sale 5th March 2004

A Mother's Day Gift

A collection of brand-new romances just for you!

Margaret Way
Anne Ashley
Lucy Monroe

On sale 5th March 2004

Available at most branches of WHSmith, Tesco, Martins, Borders, Eason, Sainsbury's and all good paperback bookshops.

0304/024/MB90V2

FREE!

4 Books
and a surprise gift!

We would like to take this opportunity to thank you for reading this Mills & Boon® book by offering you the chance to take FOUR more specially selected titles from the Modern Romance™ series absolutely FREE! We're also making this offer to introduce you to the benefits of the Reader Service™—

★ FREE home delivery
★ FREE gifts and competitions
★ FREE monthly Newsletter
★ Books available before they're in the shops
★ Exclusive Reader Service discount

Accepting these FREE books and gift places you under no obligation to buy; you may cancel at any time, even after receiving your free shipment. Simply complete your details below and return the entire page to the address below. *You don't even need a stamp!*

YES! Please send me 4 free Modern Romance books and a surprise gift. I understand that unless you hear from me, I will receive 6 superb new titles every month for just £2.60 each, postage and packing free. I am under no obligation to purchase any books and may cancel my subscription at any time. The free books and gift will be mine to keep in any case.

P4ZEE

Ms/Mrs/Miss/Mr ....Initials...............................
BLOCK CAPITALS PLEASE

Surname...

Address..

....

....Postcode ....

Send this whole page to:
UK: The Reader Service, FREEPOST CN81, Croydon, CR9 3WZ
EIRE: The Reader Service, PO Box 4546, Kilcock, County Kildare (stamp required)

Offer not valid to current Reader Service subscribers to this series. We reserve the right to refuse an application and applicants must be aged 18 years or over. Only one application per household. Terms and prices subject to change without notice. Offer expires 30th May 2004. As a result of this application, you may receive offers from Harlequin Mills & Boon and other carefully selected companies. If you would prefer not to share in this opportunity please write to The Data Manager at the address above.

Mills & Boon® is a registered trademark owned by Harlequin Mills & Boon Limited.
Modern Romance™ is being used as a trademark.
The Reader Service™ is being used as a trademark.